A STRANGER ON SHORE

A STRANGER ON SHORE

WILDA HURST KNIGHT

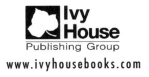
Ivy
House
Publishing Group

www.ivyhousebooks.com

PUBLISHED BY IVY HOUSE PUBLISHING GROUP
5122 Bur Oak Circle, Raleigh, NC 27612
United States of America
919-782-0281

ISBN: 1-57197-332-X
Library of Congress Control Number: 2002105330

Printed in the United States of America

To my husband, Dr. Curtis H. Knight, for his patience, encouragement, and devotion.

To my three children, Basil J. Hurst, Barbara Hurst Dameron, and William Lane Hurst.

To my devoted granddaughters, Devon Hurst and Barbara Joe Dameron, for taking the kinks out of my computer, and for handling the mailing of my material, et cetera.

To all my relatives and friends . . . you know who you are.

Acknowledgements

Laurie Rosin of Sarasota, Florida, for guiding me in the right direction.

Allen and Rita Leubeck for their encouragement.

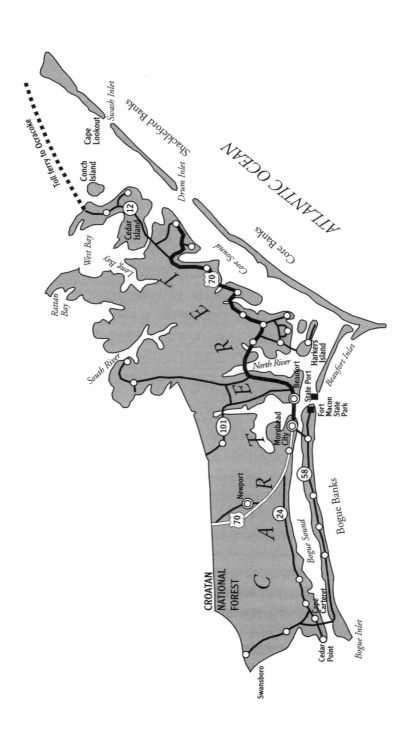

CHAPTER ONE

Bogue Banks, North Carolina

It was the gray dawn of morning as Delia slipped out of the cabin, leaving her young son, Will, asleep. Trudging up a large dune, she reached the top just as the sun peeped over the horizon. From there she saw her destination, the Bogue Inlet Lifesaving Station. Tomorrow, she thought, they will take us off this godforsaken island.

Shading her eyes with her hands, she gazed out to sea. She was oblivious to the fog tumbling across the ocean toward her, the surf's rhythmical roar, and the swirls of sand nudging her feet. Her thoughts were focused far to the east. "Oh God," she cried. "If I had listened to Papa I would be home in London with my family now. Will I ever see them again?"

Wiping away a tear, she hiked her frock above her waist and, sinking in sand to her knees, plowed down the dune. At the bottom she gathered small pieces of driftwood to start a fire to cook their morning meal.

Stacking the wood by the banked coals from the last fire, she took a kettle hanging from a tree limb and walked the short distance to the pond for water to make the fish stew.

Bullfrogs croaked their disapproval as she filled the kettle with water. Stirring the coals, she added pine straw and twigs. The straw, damp from the fog, smoldered, sending spirals of white smoke above the treetops.

Fernie Humphrey, a farmer on the mainland side, must have seen the smoke in the vicinity of his hunting cabin, for he poled his skiff across the sound to investigate. Pulling the skiff's bow ashore, he followed an overgrown trace toward the cabin. Breaking clear of the vegetation, he froze. A red-headed woman and a small boy squatted near a kettle hanging beneath a crude tripod over a smoldering fire.

"We must hurry and extinguish this fire, before someone on the mainland sees the smoke and comes snooping," said Delia, scooping fish stew with a hollowed-out gourd from the kettle onto Will's plate. "I saw the lifesaving station up the beach. They will take us to Swansboro, where we will somehow make our way—"

"Mama!" screamed Will, dropping his plate in the sand and pointing to a tree in back of her. "There's a man peeping at us!"

Delia turned and saw a tall, willowy, middle-aged man with a white goatee stride toward them. She quickly pushed Will behind her.

"I'll not harm you," the man said, smiling.

"Who are you and what do you want?" Delia asked.

"You are on my property, and that is my duck hunting camp," he said, pointing to the hut beside the pond. "That allows me to ask the first questions. How did you get here? What is your name?"

"My name is Delia O'Dare Sutton and this is my son William," she said, stooping to pick up his plate. "We came ashore when the mail boat sank."

"I'm Fernie Taylor. That boat sank three days ago and farther up the island. Have you been camping here all this time, and what is that you are cooking in my kettle?"

"We have been here two days. We caught several fish with a small discarded fishnet we found around the shore."

"You're a resourceful young woman," Fernie said. "Let's exchange the use of my cabin and equipment for you telling me where you came from and why a lovely young lady and son are camping on Bogue Banks."

"It's a long story, Mr. Taylor," she said, dishing more food onto Will's plate.

"I have all day, so start at the beginning."

I have to trust someone, Delia thought. She sat on the sand by a pine tree, leaned back against its trunk, closed her eyes and thought, *Where should I start?* After a few minutes of silence she became engrossed in her life story.

CHAPTER TWO

London, England. Years earlier.

Delia O'Dare was born in London, England in 1872, the youngest daughter of strict middle-class, God-fearing parents. Her father, a red-headed Irishman, owned and operated a popular pub in London and a small farm on the edge of town. He often scolded her for being far too credulous, adventurous and independent for a young girl. Her family and friends were unaware of her fascination for the city docks.

One afternoon when she was eighteen years old, she left home on the pretext of visiting a girlfriend. Out of sight of the house, she lifted her skirt to her knees, showing pantaloons that caused heads to turn as she dashed toward the wharf on the River Thames.

The hustle and bustle of stevedores loading and unloading ships' cargo from other countries captivated her. Exotic spices from India, perfume from France, animal hides from Africa and rugs from China could be seen in all directions. She often conversed with the fishmongers, who spent much of their days shouting out their commodities.

Strolling along the docks that balmy afternoon, she lost track of time before she suddenly realized the hour was late and it was almost dusk. She hurried along the wharf toward home. Just as she reached the street that would take her away from the waterfront, two arms grabbed her from behind, covered her mouth, pushed her in an alley and threw her to the ground. She recognized the face of a sailor from one of the ships. She struggled, but he was too strong. The last thing she remembered was the pungent smell of chloroform, and then darkness.

When she regained consciousness she was confined in a fishy-smelling gunnysack and had an awful headache. She noticed a rocking sensation, and caught the smell of hay and the offensive odor of horse manure. Working her way clear of the sack, she discovered her pantaloons were missing and there was dried blood on her legs. "Oh my God! Oh my God!" she cried as it dawned on her that she had been raped.

She worked her way through bales of hay to the deck, searching for a way to escape. Suddenly, the horses neighed. Descending the ladder was a short black man with kinky salt and pepper hair, wearing a dingy white apron. As she rushed back to her hiding place she heard the man say, "Hush now, I's going to feed you. But fust I must remove the shit from the stalls." Taking up a shovel, he scooped manure into a barrel.

When he picked up a pitchfork to give the horses hay, Delia thought she better let him know she was there or she would get a tail full of prongs. "Wait mister, I'll get out of your way," she said, springing up from the back of a bale of hay.

"Oh, Laud Gaud Jesus!" the man said, falling back into the barrel of manure. "Is you one of dem mermaids I hears the sailors talk about?"

All Delia could see of him were the whites of his eyes as he slowly peeked over the top of the barrel. "No, I'm not a mermaid," she said. "I was attacked and abducted by an ugly looking sailor with a long scar running down the side of his face, greasy hair in a ponytail, and meaty lips that reminded me of nightcrawlers. He must be the one who put me aboard. If my father finds him he will surely go to the gallows. Will you please help me get ashore?"

"I can't milady, we been underway for thirty minutes. My name is Rufus. Don't worry—me thinks me know who did it. He's always in trouble. He's a mean man, that one. But I hear he got his comeuppance late last evening in a waterfront fight. I hear he was kilt dead as a doornail; guess he feeding crabs in de bay now." He stopped to pitch hay in one of the stalls. "You's better stay hid, cause a good-looking gal would fare sorta common amongst these here white sailors. They don't show womenfolk any mercy. I'll look to your needs until we get to Charleston, South Carolina; that's in America. I's taking these here horses to Marse Maxwell. He sent me to London to fetch 'em—they prize horses."

"Oh God, Rufus, America is across the ocean and so far from home. What is the name of the ship we're on?" Delia asked.

"She named *Albatross*. I mus' go. I's the cook so I'll see you have plenty to eat."

Rufus brought her supper that evening and found her vomiting and white as a ghost. He returned topside and brought back a potion. "Drink dis milady, it will cure yer seasickness."

"Oh God! I'm dying," she cried, reaching for the bucket and vomiting.

"Here, sip this here concoction." Rufus handed her a mug. She took a whiff. "Pew! What is it?"

"It's an ol' Southern remedy of sassafras oil, rum and vinegar. It'll be a while afore ye have yer sea legs."

For weeks the ship skirted several European countries, stopping at seaports to take aboard fresh water and lemons to prevent scurvy. There was no way for Delia to escape, however, as half the the crew always stayed aboard and lounged around the top deck and gang plank.

True to his word, Rufus brought her water and food stolen from the ship's galley, and dumped her waste, along with the horses', overboard. Sometimes late at night he slipped her water for bathing.

One day Delia awoke feeling unusually nauseous. At first she thought it was seasickness again, but it wasn't quite the same. *Oh my God!* she thought. *I must be pregnant.*

When Rufus came down to bring her breakfast and feed the horses, he found her crying. "What's the trouble milady, has one of dem sailors been down here?"

"No one has been down but you, Rufus. I think I'm pregnant, and it has to be by that awful sailor."

"Dat's all right milady, when we reaches Charleston, my bossman Mr. Maxwell will know jest what to do. He one fine man. He'll help you return home."

Delia thought she would go mad confined in the dimly lit, manure-smelling hole. She had nothing to do but talk to the horses and listen to the sails flapping when they lost wind and the moaning and creaking of the hull under full sail. She thought of home, her parents and how they would accept her pregnancy. The only time she breathed fresh air was when Rufus had night watch and she could sit in the hatchway. When a sailor came topside Rufus warned her and she scurried back to her hiding place.

A few weeks later Rufus hurried down the ladder. "Milady, we's tying up at the island of Bermuda for the night. Our next port is Charleston."

"Oh Rufus! Bermuda is a British colony. If I can slip ashore maybe I can find an English family that will take me in, once they learn what happened. From there I can catch one of His Majesty's ships back to London."

"We can sho' try, but it must be after the crew has gone ashore for their usual rowdy drinking and women chasing. I'll let you know when it's safe to leave."

Minutes seemed like hours to Delia. *Maybe the crew didn't have shore leave,* she imagined, among other things. Sometime later she heard the hatch cover open and held her breath until Rufus appeared on the ladder.

"Let's go milady; we must hurry. All the crew left except the night watchman. You mus' take off your shoes."

Creeping beneath the poop deck, they often stopped and huddled in its shadow while the guard made his rounds above them. They were a few feet from the gangplank when suddenly Delia's heart skipped a beat. Four members of the crew were weaving down the wharf, herded along by bobbies carrying nightsticks. Snatches of vulgar songs filled the air. Delia and Rufus made a dash back to her hiding place in the forward hull, defeated. *Oh God, what am I going to do?* she thought. *That was my last chance to return home. I have no relatives or friends in America or money to pay my way back to England.* Crawling back on her bed of hay, she cried herself to sleep.

Two days out of Bermuda the ship begin to roll and lurch more than usual.

"Rufus, are we headed into a storm?" she asked when he brought her breakfast that morning.

"Well, I hear the captain say we in for a blow and he's batten down the hatches. But don't you worry milady, I think it's jest a nor'easter mullet blow."

Sometime later Rufus hurried down the ladder. "Milady, this ain't no mullet blow. The captain, he say the barometer has dropped fast and we's off course, near Diamond Shoals— that's off the North Carolina coast—and they's mean. Caused many a ship to sink or break up and wash ashore. I mus' see to the horses."

A short time later the creaking and groaning of the bulkhead increased as the ship rolled and pitched with the howling wind and high waves.

"Oh God! Rufus, I don't know how much more this ship can take," Delia said as she braced for each onslaught.

Before Rufus could soothe her, the horses broke free of their harnesses and began kicking the port side of the ship. Delia and Rufus tried to restrain them but were thrown around like sacks of potatoes.

"When the horses break out," said Rufus, "grab one by the tail and hang on. He'll swim ashore and take you with him. I seen a lighthouse when I's on the upper deck, and the cap'n, he say it must be near Cape Lookout, so we can't be too fer from sho'."

Minutes later, the ship rose straight up on a huge wave, slipped down into its trough, and began to break up. The port side of the vessel caved in where the horses had weakened its timbers. As the horses made a dash for the hole, Delia and Rufus each grabbed one by its tail and swam with them clear of the sinking vessel.

Several minutes later Delia crested a wave and saw a thin line of land that seemed miles away. When she couldn't see Rufus or the third horse, she panicked.

"Oh God, I'm not going to make it. Mama, Papa, and my beau Ralph will never know what happened to me!" she cried as she struggled to keep her grip on the horse's tail and her head above water. Suddenly the horse touched bottom and lurched forward, causing her to lose her grip on his tail. After being turned head over heels several times in the shore breakers, a huge wave swept her ashore, where she lay coughing up salt water.

Sometime later she saw, a short distance from shore, the keel of a ship protruding from a sand dune. Crawling to the leeward side of the wreck, she lay exhausted, listening to the wind howl and the waves crash on shore.

Delia awoke with the sun in her eyes and a quiet breeze on her face. The storm had passed and as she gazed at the rolling waves, she struggled to concentrate on what she should do next. Did Rufus make it ashore? What would she discover on this strange piece of land? With her eyes focused on the breakers, she saw something rise and fall with the waves. When it floated near she saw it was a body floating facedown. "Oh God, don't let it be Rufus," she shouted.

Wading into the surf, she pulled the body ashore. It wasn't Rufus. It was a white man about her size. *He must be one of the crewmen from the sunken schooner,* she thought. With repugnance she stripped him of his knickers and shirt, and laid them on the sand to dry. They would replace her tattered and salt-encrusted clothes. With the help of the outgoing tide, she managed to push the body back out to sea.

A number of the ship's horses had made it safely to shore. Her favorite horse, the one she named Duke, followed her to the water's edge.

Finding the water salty, he shook his head and neighed.

"All right, old boy, I'm thirsty and hungry too," she said. "Let's see what this place has to offer in the way of water, food, and shelter. I hope the natives are friendly."

She used her clothes to make reins for what was left of Duke's halter, and rode down the beach. The only life she saw were seagulls screeching as they dove into schools of small fish near shore.

Suddenly Duke lunged, almost throwing Delia off his back as he headed for the sand dunes. From the top of a dune she had a panoramic view of the area. In a ravine on the other side of the dune she saw the other two horses, grazing around a pond surrounded by scrub oaks and lush vegetation. Duke evidently heard the horses or sensed fresh water.

"Oh no!" Delia cried. "There are the horses, but I don't see Rufus; he didn't make it. I'm alone in a foreign country." Wiping away tears, she saw a large river grooved with green marsh grass that reminded her of a moth-eaten carpet.

"We must be on an island," she said to Duke as he rushed down the dune toward the pond. After drinking a fill of fresh water, she washed her salty, grimy body. While washing the sailor's dirty knickers she found several English pounds and three sixpence. Placing them with the clothes on a log to dry, she wondered if they were of any value in America.

Later in the afternoon she put on the sailor's pants and shirt—which weren't completely dry—and led Duke through a dense undergrowth of sea oats, myrtle and yaupon bushes. They reached the sound side. Across the large body of water she could barely make out the outlines of a farmhouse and dock. *Forging the grass-choked river will be dangerous,* she thought. *The only thing to do is see if anyone lives on the island.*

With the setting sun in her face she rode west along the shore; seeing nothing but shore birds and sand dunes, she turned back east. In the sunset's afterglow she saw, in the distance, a light high in the sky. "Oh Duke, that must be the Cape Lookout light Rufus told me about." She urged Duke into a full gallop, scattering ghost crabs along the way and causing flocks of gulls to take flight. When she drew near the light, she encountered a large inlet separating the two islands.

With Duke at her heels she ran up and down the shore, waving her arms and shouting, trying her best to attract someone's attention. She finally gave up when it became too dark to see. *I must wait until morning and try again,* she thought.

The calm at twilight brought sand gnats out of their hiding places in droves. They invaded her hair, nose, and eyes. She made for the ocean, but when she emerged from the water, gnats still surrounded her. With the help of a large conch shell, she dug a trench at the foot of a sand dune, deep enough to cover her body. The drowned sailor's shirt made a makeshift tent to cover her face.

"Guess I outfoxed you, you pests," she said as she settled in for the night. The mild waves lapping on shore lulled her to sleep.

The sun was peeping over the horizon when she awoke to someone yelling on the sound side of the island.

"Get ready, here they come. Cast off! She is a big one; run her wide."

Crawling out of her sand bed, Delia ran around the point of beach and saw five men. One man was standing on a high, crudely constructed platform a short distance down the shore, waving his arms and doing the shouting. "By Jove boys, she's one big school of mullets. We'll live it up tonight."

Two of the men were rowing hard toward the center of the sound, trailing a net from the stern of a skiff. They made a wide circle and headed back toward shore. Mullets were jumping everywhere—over the net, and even into the boat.

Before the skiff was beached she saw the men jump overboard and pull the net toward shore, assisted by the two on the opposite end. When the net was almost on shore one of the men stood up to relieve himself. Turning away from the shore, he saw Delia standing a few yards away. He became entangled in his breeches, fell over backwards in the net and disappeared, entangled among fish and net.

When they finally rescued him the oldest man said, "Damn you woman, look what you did. Almost caused Dink to drown, and embarrassed him with his breeches down. We lost many fish and they were full of roe. Where in the hell did you come from, dressed like a sailor? Our womenfolk don't wear sech a get-up."

His voice sounded threatening, causing Delia to step back a few feet.

"My good man, I don't give a darn about your fish. And as far as Dink, as you called him, is concerned, he has nothing I would write home about!"

They all laughed, except the one she addressed, and they returned to detangling their fish from the net. One of the men kept glancing up, smiling. She approached him and asked, "Could I have a fish? Except for a few wild berries, I haven't eaten for two days, since I landed on this island after the ship sank."

The fishermen immediately stopped removing the gilled fish from the net and looked at her, some with their mouths open, as if confused and full of disbelief.

"My God!" said one of the men. "The lifesaving station crew said there was only one survivor from that shipwreck, and he is black."

"That must be Rufus!" Delia cried. "Where is he? Please take me to him."

The men must have thought she was daft, being friendly with a black man. They told her she had landed on Shackleford Banks and they would contact the lifesaving station on Cape Lookout when they returned home to Harkers Island.

They threw her three fish, along with matches in a stained tobacco pouch, then hurriedly gathered their nets and fish. Then they shoved off, rowing hard toward home. *Like the devil was after them,* thought Delia.

She stood with her arms around Duke's neck and watched until they were out of sight. "Come Duke, let's go to the pond and cook these fish."

While the horses grazed, she cooked the fish by threading them through their gills with a stick and holding them over the fire. After eating she called Duke and rode back to the inlet to watch for the lifesaving boat. When she wasn't walking along the shore she rested on a nearby log. Soon, it was almost dark.

"Duke, I'm beginning to think those fishermen didn't contact the lifesaving station. Maybe they don't plan to rescue me." Despondent, she started to walk away, leading Duke. *Wait, there's a noise, something besides the lapping of the gentle waves. Is it my imagination,* she thought, *or is that oars I hear slapping the water?* She stood still and listened as the sound grew close. Soon she saw a boat coming toward her in the moonlight. As it slowly approached, she tried to see if Rufus was aboard. Surely they would have told him, and he would've come with them. But the two men aboard were white.

"Where is Rufus? Is he all right?" she asked.

"Yes ma'am," one man said, stepping ashore. "But he is in a mighty bad way. He was almost dead when we found him floating on a barrel half-full of horse manure. His left leg was cut mighty bad and he lost right much blood."

Seeing Duke standing behind her, he continued, "Now I know why that black man keeps talking about horses and saving the white lady as he drifts in and out of his head. Come, woman, we must hurry back to the cape. My name is Luther and this here is Seth."

She hugged Duke's neck. "I hate to leave you and the mares, but there is plenty of fresh water and grass. Someday, somehow, I will return for you."

The men hardly beached the boat at the cape before Delia bolted ashore and ran toward the crewmen's quarters. It was dark inside the two-room, roughly constructed cabin.

"Rufus! Rufus!" she called. When he didn't answer, she looked for a light and found an oil lamp and matches on a driftwood stump near the door. Lighting the lamp, she saw Rufus on a small cot in the back of the room. Rushing over to him she said, "Rufus, please answer me."

He opened his eyes and mumbled, "Laud Gaud Jesus, milady, is that really you? Thank the Laud, thank the Laud. Did the horses make it ashore?"

"Yes, I left them on an island on the other side of the inlet. How is your leg? Why didn't you stay with the horse?"

"My leg was cut when a wave knocked me close to her hoofs just as she kicked. I let go and grabbed a barrel floating close by. It kept me afloat until the lifesaving men found me."

Delia felt his forehead and realized he had a fever. "Rufus, your leg is infected."

"I's feels mighty po'ly and my leg hurts, but I am alive, thank the Laud." He closed his eyes and said no more.

Searching for something to doctor his leg, she found a box under a bunk bed containing sulfur, spirit of turpentine and rags.

She removed the smelly bandage from around his leg and shuddered. The wound was deep, red and full of pus. Remembering how her father doctored her cut foot when it was infected, she went to work. After washing the wound inside and out with turpentine, she applied the sulfur into the cut and tore a sheet to make a bandage for his leg.

By the time the lifesaving men had secured the boat and stored their gear, Delia had finished dressing Rufus' wound. She observed the sparsely furnished room containing four homemade corn-husked-bottom chairs, a tin stove, and a tree stump for a table. Against one wall were four narrow bunkbeds. *That's where the four seamen sleep,* she thought, and walked into the kitchen. On top of a wood-burning stove something was simmering in an iron pot. She lifted the lid. "Ugh! What's this gray smelly stuff?"

"That's conch stew," said one of the men as he walked in the door. "You may not like it, but that conch concoction will make old men horny and the dead rise again." Delia was amused at the way the men expressed things.

Rufus' leg slowly mended. Luther tended to his personal needs and Delia dressed his leg and fed him.

Delia's cooking was usually comprised of various types of seafood, which the crew caught, as well as sea kale she found on the beach. She prepared more combinations of food than she thought possible. Sometimes the supply boat brought other food—mostly salt pork, dried beans and cornmeal. Occasionally one of the men's wives sent over home-canned vegetables that were shared. The crewmen made sure she hid every time the supply boat came, since women weren't allowed on the cape.

After several months on the cape, Delia and Rufus became the subject of considerable gossip among the men. Their friendship was controversial, especially since there were no blacks on the islands. At first the men tolerated the two and stayed out of their way when possible. But they were not above having a little fun talking about them.

One day when Delia was walking the beach one of the men made the remark, "You know, that baby she is carrying might be that darkie's. They are awful thick. She has never told us about herself, and all we know is she is from England and was shipwrecked."

Another crewman added, "Wonder what color it will be, black or white."

"Hush your mouth, boys," Luther said. "I don't give a damn what color it is: black, white, cream, or the color of mullet roe. I like her; she has spunk, that gal does. She has learned to cook a mean pot of vittles and cornbread. Better'n any of us can. Besides, she is sure a good-looking gal."

Two months later, while the lifesaving men were scraping barnacles from the rescue boat's bottom, they again discussed Delia's pregnancy.

"Boys, looks like the lady will spawn any day now," said Luther. "It's too dangerous to have the midwife from the island come over here, or her go there. The rumors would fly around like wildfire. They will swear that baby belongs to one of us, and as for you, Doodle, you'd be in deep shit. Hattie will mellow yer head with her left-handed conch shell, like the time she caught ye messing around with Dink's wife. Yer head is still knotty."

Doodle rubbed his head. "Yeah, we better go look for Rufus and see what he says."

They found him on the beach side of the lighthouse, fishing for drum. Rufus listened to their predicament. When they had finished, he laughed, "Don't ye worry, boys. I will bring dat youngern into the world. I have done this many times with darkies around Charleston. I guess ye could call me a midman when dere won't a midwife near. I 'spects it will be soon by the—" He was interrupted when a fish almost took the fishing pole out of his hands. He landed a large bass and laid it on the beach beside several more before continuing.

"That ol' moon will be full next week. That's the time when she will birth that youngern. They usually drop on the full of the moon. A baby is like an apple—it won't fall until it's ripe. Everything is ready. By the way, I tore up two of your bedsheets, to stanch the blood and bind the navel after I cut the umbilical cord, without asking you. Sorry."

Delia, unfamiliar with childbirth, was apprehensive when the time drew near for her delivery. And for the first time since she arrived on the island, she wished for a woman to confide in.

The harvest moon always seems larger and closer to Earth than at other times of the year, and the full moon on this early October evening was no exception. It hung over the cape and gradually changed from a huge orange ball to a misty white disk as it slowly ascended.

During the night the men were awakened by a scream. "Jest as I said, she going to drop that youngern this night," said Rufus.

The crewmen made a dash for the door, kicking up sand as they ran toward the lighthouse.

"Oh God, Rufus, it hurts something awful, and I am wet clear to my toes."

"That would be your water broke, milady. It won't be long now afore ye birth that youngern, sho'nuff. Wish I had a box of snuff so I could snuff ye like we does at home." Rufus explained how putting snuff under the woman's nose at the last minute makes them sneeze hard. "Then out pops the youngern. Many a youngern down home has come into this world that way."

"What are you doing?" Delia asked as Rufus began to tie a rope around the foot of the cot after he cut off the sinkers and cork from a fishnet.

"I'm making ye a birthing halter. Now take a rope in each hand and the next time ye feel a pain, pull as hard as ye can on the ropes."

After a few more hard contractions, a baby girl was born. Rufus cut the cord, cleaned the baby, and put her in her mother's arms. "She has yer red hair, milady, and weighs, I recollect, seven pounds."

He left Delia, who was exhausted, and ran outside to give the crewmen the news. They were squatting around a fire eating roasted oysters and telling raunchy jokes.

"Would ya'll like to come and see the baby girl?" Rufus asked.

"What color is she?" one of the men asked.

"She's white! What in the hell color did ye think she would be?" Rufus mumbled all the way back to the cabin.

"All right boys, ante up," Luther said. "You owe me fifty cents apiece. I bet you it would be white."

The next morning Rufus asked, "What have ye named the youngern, milady?"

"I'm going to let you name her, Rufus. If you hadn't saved my life and been so kind, neither one of us would be alive today."

"Thank ye, milady, that's the kindest thing anyone has ever done for me. Could I name her after my dead mother, Loren Ward?"

"Loren Ward O'Dare is your name," Delia said, smiling at the baby in her arms.

CHAPTER THREE

It was late October, and the baby a month old, when Luther told Delia and Rufus they must leave the cape before the first of November.

"The winters on the cape can be rough due to nor'easter squalls. Bad weather will hinder the supply boat from coming, and provisions sometimes get mighty low. And also, on the third of November there will be a change of duty. We'll be replaced by another crew for six months."

"Yeah, and a good-looking white gal and a darkie ain't going to set so well with the new crew," Floyd Garner, the youngest of the crewmen, said. He never liked them being on the island.

Luther went on to say, "It's best you go to the mainland instead of the other islands. I'll send you to my friend's home in Beaufort. He's a black preacher and a good darkie. He will remember me from the many times he sold us oysters here at the cape. That's before he took up preaching."

They decided November 1 would be the date they would leave. As the hour drew near for their departure, the servicemen gave Delia and Rufus clean, somewhat worn government-issue pants and shirts, and a blanket for the baby.

"We are going to miss you," Luther said. "Don't tell where you got the clothes or we'll be in heaps of trouble." By their sad looks, Delia could tell the men hated to see them go.

They boarded the longboat with Luther at the helm, crossed the inlet, and entered a narrow channel choked with marsh grass that ran parallel to Shackleford Banks. They were close enough to see thousands of sand fiddlers guarding their burrows while constantly moving their large claws back and forth.

"Those fiddlers look like they are fiddling for a big hoedown," said Rufus, laughing.

Delia looked for the horses as they rode by. They were almost in sight of Beaufort when she saw three horses grazing near the shore and recognized Duke. "Please, Luther, could I stop and see the horses?" she asked.

"Well, just for a few minutes. I have to return before dark. It's my turn to refuel the lighthouse lamp tonight."

Delia jumped ashore and ran toward the horses, calling Duke. *He doesn't recognize me,* she thought. When the others bolted at the sight of her she saw that the mare was with colt. "Looks like the Banks will be full of ponies one of these days," she said, climbing back aboard the boat. As the boat pulled away from the shore she looked back and became teary-eyed when she saw Duke standing on a sand dune watching them.

Luther put his two passengers ashore on the edge of town and pointed northwest. "Go around Beaufort to the colored section called Shantytown, and ask for Preacher Thomas. Tell him that Luther sent you."

Heading in the direction Luther pointed, they followed an open meadow around the edge of town. From a short distance Delia saw large two-story homes, mostly painted white, with widow walks perched on their roofs. Oleanders bloomed behind white picket fences around the houses.

The scenery was different when they arrived at Shantytown, on the outskirts of Beaufort. Small, unpainted, weather-worn houses with tin roofs were clustered together along a dirt road.

They approached a black woman hoeing field peas in her small vegetable garden. "Lady, can you tell me where Preacher Thomas lives?" Rufus asked.

The woman straightened, leaned on her hoe, wiped the sweat from her brow with the tail of her apron, and looked them up and down for several minutes before she finally said, "I's don't know what's you wants the preacher fer, but if its to get married or baptized, nedder one will happen; we segregate in this here town. You must be strangers from up North. If it's marriage you after 'pears like you is might late," she said, eyeing the baby, and continued to hoe her garden.

After several more times of asking and being rebuffed, they found Preacher Thomas rocking on his front porch. Rufus pushed open an old, rickety gate hanging by one hinge, and walked to the porch. "Preacher Thomas, you don't know me, sir, but a friend of yern by the name of Luther Midget at the Cape Lookout Lifesaving Station said fer us to look you up."

The old man stared at Delia, the baby, and back to Rufus. He took his glasses off and wiped them on his shirt. "All I has to say is, der must be a good reason for him to send a white-woman, a baby, and a darkie to see me."

"Let me tell ye how and why we came to see you," said Rufus.

"Sit here on the porch and let me hear yer spiel."

Rufus told of their experiences. When he had finished, Preacher Thomas called to his wife, who had been standing behind the screen door, "Lizzie, take the woman and baby in

23

the house." Once they disappeared through the door, he said, "I was on Shackleford Banks a couple weeks ago and I was wondering where those horses came from."

"Preacher Thomas, those horses ye saw belong to Marse Maxwell of Charleston, South Carolina. I needs to let him know where they be. I would like to catch a boat heading south."

"Well, there's a freighter outta Norfolk that stops here once in awhile on it's way south. She was here a week ago; it'll be some while before another one ties up here. You can stay with Lizzie and me until you find work to pay your way to Charleston. But the lady must stay in town with white folks. They don't take too kindly with the mingling of whites and blacks, hereabouts."

Thomas paused long enough to cut two bites from a plug of tobacco. Then, after offering one to Rufus, he continued. "We will go see Mrs. Sara Willis. Her man is Cap'n Willis; he's gone overseas on a trading mission. Mrs. Sara has no youngerns; she old, po'ly and awful lonely. They's real fine white folks. I's their yard man for many years. Lizzie, she helps out in the house once in a while when O'Lent, the full-time maid, is sick or visiting her relatives down on Bogue Sound."

"Mr. Rufus, come in and have some yaupon tea," Lizzie called from the screen door.

Rufus took Delia aside and told her what Preacher Thomas said, trying to explain why she must stay in Beaufort. However, she still could not understand why she could not stay with them.

"You are in the South, milady," said Rufus.

"I don't give a darn about your Southern ways. I wish to stay here," she said.

Preacher Thomas overheard them and said, "I'm sorry. It's not only white folks—my people don't approve either," said

Preacher Thomas. "If'n ye stay with us that collection plate at my next preaching might come up lacking no matter how hard I bare down on these here Ten Commandents."

Late that afternoon, Preacher Thomas took Delia to meet Mrs. Sara. Rufus accompanied them. They walked through the vegetable garden and knocked on the back door. Mrs. Sara invited them into the kitchen, and when she saw Delia's disheveled clothing, said, "My goodness, dear, what happened to you?"

Rufus started to answer when Delia interrupted, "Rufus, for gosh sakes, let me speak for myself."

When Mrs. Sara heard Delia's story, she said "My dear, you may stay here until you decide what to do. Come, I will show you your room. There are clothes that my niece left here last summer; I'm sure they will fit you."

Walking through the house to the stairway, Delia started crying.

"Goodness, dear," said Mrs. Sara. "What's the matter? Don't you want to stay here?"

"Oh, yes, Mrs. Sara. It's just that your house and lovely furnishings remind me of my home in London. I miss my family and home so much."

"Well, child, maybe you can return home with Captain Willis the next time he has cargo bound for England." After showing her new houseguest the wash basin and wardrobe, she left Delia alone to bathe.

Delia had poured water into the wash bowl and was about to begin washing when she heard the back screen door close. Running to the window, she saw Rufus and Preacher Thomas turning the corner of the house. She hollered to Rufus to wait.

"I must go, milady. I'm going to the waterfront and see about a job on the docks. If'n you need me I will be staying with Preacher Thomas."

When she opened the chifforobe she was delighted to find three lovely morning dresses, and she chose a blue and white striped one with a sailor collar trimmed in the same blue color. It was a perfect fit.

After she nursed the baby and rocked her to sleep, she put her down for the evening and returned to the kitchen, where she saw supper being prepared by a black woman. "Oh, you must be O'Lent, the girl Preacher Thomas told me about. I'm Delia. Where is Mrs. Sara?"

"This time o' day she goes up to the widow's walk and looks out over the ocean with her spyglass, watching for Captain Willis," said O'Lent, while putting a pan of biscuits in the oven. "He sho' been gone a long time. He left five months ago for England with a cargo of turpentine and she hasn't heard hide nor hair of him since."

"How do you get up to the widow's walk?" Delia asked.

"Go down the hallway to the last door you sees on the left. You will find a narrow winding staircase that goes to the roof. Tell Mrs. Sara supper is almost done and I will be leaving shortly."

CHAPTER FOUR

Every morning and afternoon, weather permitting, Mrs. Sara and Delia were on the widow's walk scanning the horizon for a sail.

Two months passed and there was still no sign of Captain Willis or his schooner.

"I'm afraid something terrible has happened to the Captain," said Mrs. Sara as she began to cry. "His ship probably sank in a storm."

"Please don't cry, Mrs. Sara," said Delia. "He could, for some reason, be tied up in London. He'll be coming home soon."

Three days later Delia saw something on the horizon through the scope, but it was too far away to tell what it was. Afraid it was just an optical illusion, she didn't mention it to Mrs. Sara.

After supper Delia cleared the table while Mrs. Sara rocked the baby.

"Child, you have been a godsend," Mrs. Sara said. "Unable to have a child of my own, I have become very attached to you and the baby, and regardless of whether or not

Captain Willis returns, I want you to stay with me. O'Lent is getting feeble, and you have helped her so much with the household chores. I will give you room and board and a few wages." Bowing her head, she cried.

Delia took the baby from Mrs. Sara and put her arm around her shoulders. "I love you too, Mrs. Sara. You have been kind to both of us—and please don't give up on Captain Willis."

Early the next morning both were on the widow's walk. Delia used the telescope first, and saw a vessel under full sail heading toward Beaufort inlet.

"Mrs. Sara, it looks like a sailing vessel is headed toward the inlet."

"Tell me dear, does it have a foremast with its mainmast amidship, and is the hull painted black with white gunwales?"

"Yes, and she is riding high above the red water line. Looks like the ship is carrying a light cargo, if any." Delia handed Mrs. Sara the spyglass.

"Thank God! It is the *Lady Sara*, my husband's schooner. Hurry, we must go downstairs and prepare for his homecoming. We will come back this afternoon and see him come through the inlet. I would love to go down to the docks and watch them tie up. It's always an exciting time when a ship comes into the harbor, but Captain Willis won't let me go. He says the sailors use such obscene and harsh language that it's not fit for a lady's ears."

Returning to the widow's walk that afternoon, they watched the ship's sails being unfurled, all except the foremast jib. The schooner approached the inlet slowly since the swift ebbing tide made navigation across the bar tricky.

"It will be late tonight before the captain will be able to come home," said Mrs. Sara. "And it will soon be too dark to see, so we might as well go downstairs."

28

Delia was awakened around midnight by a loud banging on the door. Tiptoeing out of the room, she looked over the balustrade into the downstairs hall. She saw Mrs. Sara, holding a kerosene lamp, open the front door for two men to enter. One of them embraced Mrs. Sara, indicating to Delia which one was Captain Willis.

Turning to the man standing behind him, Captain Willis said, "Sara, this is my new first mate, Dunlap. Old Judson died while we were dockside in England and we buried him at sea, God rest his soul. I found Dunlap on the waterfront dock, where he was left for dead by the sailors on a vessel docked next to mine. They upped anchor and sailed during the night. The dockmaster said he would make a good first mate. I had him patched up and signed him on. He will stay here tonight. Tomorrow, I will outfit him with a bedroll and change of clothes. He will use the schooner for his living quarters."

Mrs. Sara held the lamp up to better see the man's face. Delia almost fainted and stumbled against the balustrade. *Oh my God,* she thought, *it's the man that raped me and put me aboard ship. I will never forget that gargoyle face and the sinister scar on his cheek.*

They looked up when they heard her stumble. "Oh," Captain Willis said, "who do we have here?"

"Aye," said Dunlap with a sneer. "A vision if I ever saw one, and I have seen it on the docks of London."

Delia quickly returned to her room, closed the door and began to pack her few belongings and two dresses from the chifforobe into a pillowcase.

"Never you mind, my late husband," said Mrs. Sara. "I have a bone or two to pick with you. Go settle your mate, then come to the kitchen and give an account of yourself—then I will tell you about Delia and her baby. But first I want to know why it has taken you so long to make this sea voyage. Looks like you came back with an empty schooner."

After the conversation died down, Delia heard Captain Willis and Dunlap come upstairs and enter the bedroom next to hers. She quickly dressed the baby, placed their clothes by the door, and waited until she thought all were asleep and it was safe to leave. Tiptoeing down the steps, she was almost to the front door when she heard Dunlap whisper, "Aye, me fancy doxy, you won't escape me this time."

Looking up, she saw him leaning over the balustrade. With the baby in one arm and clothes in the other, she ran as fast as she could toward Shantytown. Dunlap caught her just as she reached Preacher Thomas' yard gate. She started kicking and screaming for Rufus. By the time Thomas and Rufus reached the porch Dunlap had her on the ground and was trying to tie her wrist.

"Don't you niggers interfere or I'll kill you. This is my white gal and I'm taking her with me. And I bet that brat is mine 'cause she was a virgin when I laid her."

Rufus picked up a hoe from the yard and ran toward him. Dunlap, with his hands occupied trying to restrain Delia, could not ward off the attack. Rufus brought the hoe down with vigor, splitting his head open. Dunlap was dead before he fell across Delia and the baby, covering them with blood and brains.

"Oh, Laud Gaud Jesus," Rufus cried. "What do I do now? I didn't mean to kills him. I jest wanted to addle him."

Preacher Thomas, in his usual commanding way, said, "Fust, let's get the gal and baby in the house so Liz can clean them up. She can stay with us 'til we figure out what to do. Then we takes this devil's servant out of town. When we gets back, we all swears on the Good Book to tell no one what happened."

While the preacher hitched up the mule to a two-wheel cart, Rufus wrapped Dunlap's body in potato sacks.

"We better hurry, Rufus. It will soon be daylight, and we must dump him before someone sees us. There's a small creek that empties into Core Sound. It's the home of several big gators. They will make short order of this mean rascal."

Two days later, Captain Willis reported Delia and Dunlap missing and posted a twenty-five dollar reward for anyone knowing of their whereabouts.

"We must get the gal out of town," Preacher Thomas said to Rufus. "Folks will say she did away with him and left town."

"Where will she go?" Rufus asked.

"I have a friend, Clarence Tilton, who is the mail carrier for Conch Island, one of the Outer Banks islands. The only way to get there is by boat and it's a three-hour run. She'll be safe there." He had Delia write Clarence a letter asking him to take her and the baby over to the island and not tell a soul where she came from.

In the letter, Preacher Thomas promised Clarence that whenever he came to hear him preach and they passed the collection plate he wouldn't have to help the Lord for six occasions, and he'd mention him in his prayers.

Delia didn't venture outside of the house. When anyone came to visit, Preacher Thomas would answer the door, and say, "Lizzie ain't feeling up to company today, she has the vapors." He'd then close the door.

A rumor started around town that Delia and Dunlap had planned to meet in America. They said that she was a stowaway and that he posed as first mate on the *Lady Sara*. Also, it was told that they had escaped before Scotland Yard could apprehend them for some terrible crime they had committed.

Mrs. Sara was devastated over the loss of Delia and the baby. She didn't believe the vicious stories they told about her, although she couldn't account for both of them leaving during the night.

At the end of the week, Preacher Thomas received a letter from Clarence saying he would carry out the preacher's instructions. Soon after sunset the next day while Preacher Thomas and Rufus hitched the mule to the cart, Lizzie helped Delia pack her few belongings.

"Don't light the lantern," Preacher Thomas said, tying the lantern on the cart's tailgate, "until you are well out of town."

Delia didn't mention that the baby was fretful and had a slight fever when she dressed her for the trip. She didn't want to worry them.

Thanking Preacher Thomas and Lizzie for their hospitality, she kissed them good-bye. Fearful for her sick baby and the risky ride to Cedar Island, she climbed up on the wooden seat beside Rufus.

The narrow dirt road that ran east from Beaufort to Cedar Island, where she would catch the mail boat, occasionally passed the back of small fishing villages clustered together along the shoreline, all facing the ocean.

In the dark the only thing visible was the lantern, now lit, bobbing on the tailgate. The creaking cart wheel and the occasional snort of the mule were the only breaks in the silence. This was nothing unusual to the inhabitants of the area since horses and boats were their only mode of transportation. Delia hoped people would think it was one of theirs returning home after a day in Beaufort.

It seemed that every small-frame house had at least two coon or deer dogs that barked as they passed. One owner appeared at a door and hollered, "Hush yer mouth, you flea-bitten hound, or I will come out thar and fill your arse full of buckshot." All along the way they could hear dogs baying in the distance.

Two hours out of Beaufort they stopped by a small creek of brackish water. "We're a good way from town," said Rufus. "It's safe to stop and let the mule drink."

"I'm hungry," said Delia, reaching for the box of food Lizzie had prepared for them. It was filled with cornbread, sweet potatoes, fried chicken, and flat sweetcakes.

She gave the box of food to Rufus, then took the baby from the wooden box crib that Rufus and Preacher Thomas had made for her.

"Oh Rufus!" she cried. "The baby is burning up with fever."

Rufus took the baby and submerged her in the water. "This will cool her down. She just has a bug," he said, trying to soothe Delia. But he knew the baby was seriously ill. There was nothing he could do but pray, for it wasn't safe to stop and ask for assistance. He wrapped the baby in a blanket and placed her back in the box.

An hour later Delia requested they stop so she could stretch her cramped body and relieve her bladder. On the way back to the cart she suddenly smelled a strong, unfamiliar musty smell. At the same time a dark object streaked across the road in front of her. She stopped still in her tracks and started screaming. Rufus came running as fast as his short legs could carry him.

"It's gone, milady. It was a black bear being chased by them hounds—and, oh Jesus, here they comes!" he shrieked, pushing Delia back out of the way as six hound dogs crossed the road, hot on the bear's trail.

"We mus' hurry before the hunters get here. I hear 'em coming, and they's not too fer."

Back in the cart, Rufus reached down, grabbed the mule by the tail, and twisted as hard as he could.

"Rufus, what are you doing to that poor animal?"

"This is the only way I know how to make an old, stubborn mule run."

They were a good way down the road before Rufus slowed the mule to a walk.

Oh God, how much further must we go? Delia thought. *If Conch Island is anything like what we have seen along the way, I wish I had stayed in Beaufort and faced the sheriff. My rear end is numb and I need a bath.* She started counting fireflies to pass the time.

An orange glow from the rising sun suddenly appeared on the horizon as they broke out of the woods into a savanna of green marsh grass that seemed to stretch for miles in every direction.

"Oh God, Rufus, do we have to cross that vast wasteland to reach that island I see in the distance?" Delia grimaced.

"Yes. That must be Cedar Island. Preacher Thomas said we would come to this open place. All it's fit fer is to hold the world together."

Silhouetted against the pastel colors of daybreak, Delia saw hundreds of egrets perched on old, gnarled trees scattered throughout the savanna. The trees' leafless branches reached toward the sky and their roots were exposed, as if they were holding on for dear life. At intervals the muddy road crossed over logs spanning narrow, twisting estuaries that would eventually empty into the sea.

A short way from their destination Rufus stopped the mule. "Milady, we should bathe the baby to cool her fever, as this looks like the last fresh stream before we reach the island."

The scenery changed drastically when they reached Cedar Island. Water oak trees, with leathery evergreen leaves and waxy white berries, draped with Spanish moss and mistletoe, formed a canopy over the cart path. Vacant birds' nests could be seen in the trees awaiting the arrival of the spring migration.

Breaking clear of the dense growth of trees, they came upon a few clapboard shacks overlooking a long pier that jutted into Pamlico Sound. The shacks appeared to be deserted. Behind them were piles of shucked, smelly scallop and oyster shells. Off to one side, fishnets stretched between poles or trees, drying or in need of mending.

Tied along the pier were several skiffs gently being rocked by small waves which passed under their bottoms. Further down the pier Delia saw a larger boat and assumed it was Clarence and his mail boat.

Rufus tied the mule and cart in the shade of a tree. Seeing that the baby was asleep, they walked out on the pier to see if it was Clarence. On their way they saw a man on the stern sheet of a skiff who seemed to be having trouble cleaning dead crabs and seaweed from a fishnet.

"Sir, could you please tell us if that is the mail boat at the end of the pier?" Rufus asked.

"If ye ain't blind ye could see her tied up at the end of the pier," the man said with a sneer. Spitting a squirt of tobacco juice, he went back to his net.

"That bloke isn't too friendly," Delia said as they approached the clumsy-looking scow tied at the end of the pier.

The aroma of seafood came from the galley and a black face appeared from the forward hatch. "You must be the lady Preacher Thomas wrote me about. Come aboard. Any friend of the preacher is a friend of mine," he said, grinning.

"I must get my baby," said Delia. With Rufus following, she walked back to the cart.

Rufus climbed on the cart to hand Delia the baby who he thought was asleep—until he realized she wasn't breathing. Gently shaking the crib several times with no response, he touched her forehead. It was cold and clammy.

"Oh Laud Gaud Jesus! Lorna is dead."

"No! No, she can't be!" screamed Delia, running to the cart. "Give her to me." Holding the baby in her arms, she fell to her knees and rocked back and forth, crying. Hearing the commotion, Clarence came running down the pier. The man in the skiff also joined them.

They buried the baby in her box crib underneath a tall oak, a short distance from the narrow roadway they had recently passed. At Delia's request a cross was carved on the tree trunk above the grave. Clarence and Ray Meadows, the man from the skiff, gathered conch shells from around the shore and placed them in neat rows on top of the grave.

"Come, Miss Delia, we must get underway," said Clarence. "I need to return before dark for the tide will be low. The sound can be wicked on dark nights, making it hard to see the shoals."

She hardly had time to tell Rufus good-bye before the boat began to pull away from the pier. With tears running down her cheeks, she stood on the stern waving farewell until he was just a speck on the pier. It was too cool to stay outside, so she joined Clarence in the pilothouse.

CHAPTER FIVE

"Clarence, I don't see any buoys. How do you tell where the channel is?" Delia asked.

"This old flat-bottom scow doesn't draw but three feet. I can tell where the sand shoals are by the color of the water. Water over shoals is a lighter blue, and on a windy day white-crested ripples will mark their existence."

Clarence kept Delia entertained with his knowledge of the island's ethnic background, its history and legends, as well as his own experiences. Some of his graphic accounts of life as a mail carrier for twenty years were both humorous and sad.

"Folks on these islands don't cater to strangers right away," he said, turning sharply to miss a shoal. Delia immediately thought of her father's warnings back in London. She felt better, though, when he said, "You'll have a friend for life once they accept you. But it usually takes a while. They will lie for you, steal for you, and give you the shirt off their back if you need it. But don't laugh at our cockney English."

Clarence's face turned serious and his eyes narrowed. "Like one time we had a fella come down from New York. He shot his mouth off, calling us ignorant, because he had a cast net no one hereabouts had ever seen." He stopped and looked into

Delia's face. "He threw that damn net into Silver Lake, and you know what? The rope tangled around his leg and he fell smack into the net. He and that net sank out of sight."

Delia, suddenly chilled, stared at him, half-knowing what was coming.

"Somebody yelled, 'Let the bastard drown!' Nobody moved to help him. Yup, that's what happened. Everybody jest turned and walked away and left him floundering. That'll teach him to make fun of us."

She looked at him and didn't know what to say.

Two hours later Clarence slowed the boat to enter Silver Lake. Delia awoke from a miserable sleep. Mourning for her baby, she still couldn't help admiring the cozy little village. It spread across a horseshoe-shaped shoreline, with whitewashed cottages nestled beneath towering oak trees. Small sailboats and skiffs of various sizes lay on their sides in the white sand with their keels, or flat bottoms, turned up to the sun. *They look like huge dead fish,* thought Delia.

"They're left like that for the sun to kill the barnacles. Then they are scraped clean, corked and put back in the water," said Clarence. "And those wooden racks you see are for drying fishnets."

Looking south, Delia saw a small lighthouse jutting out in the sound.

"What a small lighthouse; it's all white with no markings like the others I've seen," she said.

"The islanders like to boast that it's the oldest and smallest lighthouse on the North Carolina coast, but I have heard it's the second one," said Clarence as he turned the boat sharply toward the dock.

When they drew near the village dock Delia saw people gathered there watching them arrive.

"They're looking forward to their mail, any news from the mainland, and the few supplies they requested on my previous trip," Clarence said, blowing the boat whistle

The boat eased broadside to the dock. Delia stepped from the cabin just as a young boy jumped aboard with a rope to help Clarence tie up. He stood with the rope in his hands and stared until a man on the dock said, "All right, Tim boy, quit looking at that redhead and help Clarence unload."

"That's Percy Tyndall," Clarence whispered to Delia. "The self-appointed postmaster. He attended two years of high school somewhere on the mainland, and he thinks he's the island's mayor and judge. He is also owner of the only general store on the island. Stay clear of him—he thinks he is a woman's man."

When the boat was secured to the dock and the few boxes put ashore, Clarence introduced Delia to Percy and then asked if he knew of someone with whom she could work for in exchange for room and board.

Percy looked Delia over from head to foot. "My Gaud boys, she has a flare in her bow and a round stern equal to a Harker's Island boat. And her legs ain't no set-net stakes either. She should be called 'Red' after that full head of purty red hair."

Delia started to tell him where to go, but decided to ignore the remark, afraid she would alienate someone and later regret having done so.

Percy stared at Delia a few minutes before he answered Clarence. "If she can read or write, which I doubt, old Miss Lucy lives alone and needs someone to help with the housework and write letters. She hates doing both."

That did it for Delia. "Mr. Tyndall, sir! I think I surpass you when it comes to education; your manners are deplorable and, in general, your deportment purely stinks. No offense intended, and if you would be so kind, I would like to meet Miss Lucy." She shook hands with Clarence. "Thank you so much, Clarence, for the safe trip and the information you gave me. I shall not forget the forewarning, and look forward to your next trip.

"Take care, Miss Delia. I shall keep Preacher Thomas' promise—my lips are sealed," said Clarence.

"Mr. Tyndall, I will see you on shore," said Delia. She turned her back toward him and, with her head held high, walked off the pier.

"Damn, whar did you pick up that hot filly, Clarence?" asked Percy. "She acts like she has a wild briar up her tail."

Ignoring him, Clarence helped the men shove the boat clear of the dock for the return to the mainland.

His leaving was a cue for Percy to put on the pious look of postmaster and pass out the few letters and cards to a handful of recipients. Except for emergencies, which were sent and received by Morse code from the lifesaving station, letters from the mainland were the island's main means of communication. Those that received letters shared them with those that didn't. The few that couldn't read were read to by those that could—providing they were on speaking terms that week.

The house where Percy took Delia was typical of those on the island—except for the outhouse, where Delia stopped first. Percy said it was the envy of the island. She opened the door to the privy, which had a wooden floor. A fancy kerosene chandelier that could be raised and lowered by a chain hung from the ceiling. Several vases of paper roses adorned two sides, and in one corner an ornate English brass coal bucket held old editions of the Farmer's Almanac. Delia later heard it wasn't uncommon for two women to sit inside for an hour, dip their snuff, and gossip.

Delia knocked on the door of the house and a woman's voice said, "For Gaud's sake, come on in. What you knocking fer, nobody on the island knocks. Ye must be a stranger on shore."

Delia entered a rustic, but neat and cozy, room. An elderly woman with a raccoon on her lap sat in a large ornate rocker with a brass cuspidor by her side. The chair had been placed in front of a fireplace made of stones that Delia later learned were ship ballast, dumped ashore by ships from foreign countries. Hanging over the fireplace mantle, and dominating the entire room, was a baroque-framed, full length oil painting of a cynical looking woman dressed in Elizabethan style.

"Miss Lucy, this here is Delia O'Dare," said Percy. "She would like to board with you and work for her keep." He paused. "Now Miss Lucy, none of yer salty talk. She is a lady, and I don't think she has ever heard some of the talk you can come up with."

"Get the hell outta here, Percy, afore I sic my raccoon on you." Turning to Delia she said, "Honey, sit down here across from me so I can eyeball you."

Anxious to be left alone with Delia, Miss Lucy noticed Percy was taking his time leaving yet doing his best to appear disinterested. "Gets, I said, you rambunctious horny ol' toad." By then Percy was halfway out the door.

"Now chile, let's talk," said Miss Lucy. "And ye watch out for that skirt-chasing ol' fool, Percy. I saw him eyeballing ye. I can see and hear better'n these fools around here think I can. I learn a lot that way."

When Miss Lucy stopped talking long enough to dig in her apron pocket for her snuffbox and brush, Delia observed the woman before her. *She must be in her late seventies.* Her black and silver streaked hair, strangely similar to the pet raccoon's, parted in the middle and twisted into a bun at the nape of her neck. Over a long dress that reached her ankles, she wore a neat, white apron. Her face was wrinkled and weathered-looking, but the twinkle in her bright blue eyes indicated humor and alertness.

"Now chile, tell me about yerself, whar ye came from, and how ye happened to wind up on this island."

Delia didn't know why, but intuition told her she could trust this woman. She told her everything, from her abduction on the waterfront of England until now, including the reward for her.

Miss Lucy quietly listened to every word, and showed feelings of sympathy for Delia when she said, "Honey chile, ye have been momicked. Yer life will be a secret between the two of us. I'll be happy to give ye room and board as long as ye conduct yerself in a proper manner and keep yer skirts clean— no fiddle-faddling around the island. You can move into the room on the right side of the hall."

Their conversation continued on for several more hours, and included Miss Lucy's life history.

She told Delia she was born at Portsmouth, Virginia. When she was sixteen she met her husband, Benny Jenkins. At that time he was stationed at Portsmouth with the lifesaving station.

"I tell you, honey, that man plum swept me off my feet. We ran away when he was transferred to the Cape Lookout Lifesaving Station. That is how I wound up on Conch Island. This was also Benny's home, and it's whar he is buried."

She stopped reminiscing when the raccoon jumped from her lap and trotted to the door.

"Honey chile, will you please let Sooner out?"

"What an unusual name for an animal," said Delia, going to the door.

"I call him Sooner 'cause he'd jest as soon pee on the floor as not. Now he has to either pee or go courting. He's getting too old for courting—but he thinks he is still a young stud."

Delia returned to the chair across from Miss Lucy and asked her to continue.

"Well, five years after we moved in this house, Benny was lost at sea while on a rescue mission. His body washed ashore five days later. He tol' me several times that he wanted to be buried in the front yard. 'That way I will be near you,' he said.

His grave and headstone are out thar," she said as she pointed out the window, "under that large, live oak tree—not an uncommon location. Nearly every home on the island has their own cemetery, in the front or back yard."

Miss Lucy paused momentarily. "Chile, I was thinking about the British cemetery whar ten English soldiers were buried when they washed up on the beach during the American Revolution. After the war, England paid the state for the cemetery lot and hired someone to maintain it. The British flag flies daily over a white picket fence surrounding the graves. So, ye see, chile, ye have a little piece of yer home-land right here on the island."

I wonder if one of the sailors could be my ancestor, thought Delia.

"Ye can move into yer room, chile, while I go spring a leak. I have to go real often these days."

While she was gone Delia had a chance to observe the room's artifacts. The furniture was obviously very old and well crafted. On a small marble tabletop were several daguerreo-type pictures.

When Miss Lucy returned, she saw Delia staring at an elaborate and ornate dueling saber hanging on a wall.

"That saber belonged to the captain of a Spanish galleon. Benny's mother said it was found in a trunk that washed ashore after the galleon met its fate on Frying Pan Shoals." She went on to say, "Many of these artifacts belonged to Benny's mother. They were taken from wrecks or abandoned vessels from other countries, mostly England." Miss Lucy smiled and continued, "I heard that during the revolution an English mil-itary schooner ran aground during a storm and broke up. Among the debris that floated ashore were several chests of military uniforms. The next day people said the island looked like an English battalion with all the men dressed in battle array."

That shipwreck reminded her of her favorite story. Without breaking stride, she continued. "One summer we had one of those roving hellfire and brimstone preachers come to the island for a revival week of soul saving. Preachers are scarce as hen's teeth on the island. That suits me jest fine. He worked on the non-members, trying to get them to come to the altar and be saved. He preached and raved on and on until a few timid souls went up. One came from the back of the church carrying a note that read: 'Times is hard, we ain't had a shipwreck in three years. Stop yer yacking and pray for a ship, or else.' Not knowing what the 'else' entailed, the preacher prayed, 'Oh Lord, I don't want anything bad to happen to anyone, but for God's sake send them a shipwreck or they will perish. Amen and amen."

The next morning a three-mast schooner lay foundered on a shoal. The lifesaving crew rescued the men aboard, and the ship was left to the islanders. That evening, men, women and children joined the church. Religion flourished for about two months; after that, they were right back to cussin', lyin', and fornicatin' agin."

Delia laughed, amused by Miss Lucy's strong Eastern dialect, and wondered how much of what Miss Lucy was telling was true, exaggerated, or just made up. It really didn't matter because she hadn't laughed like this since she left London.

She glanced up at the oil painting above the mantle. "Is that lovely painting a relative of yours, Miss Lucy?

"Heavens no. That is Theodosius Burr, Aaron Burr's daughter. It's been in the Jenkins family for years, and it's one of my prized possessions. I was tol' it's very valuable."

Delia looked at the picture which provoked thoughts on the way Theodosius was believed to have died. Seems Theodosius had her portrait painted for her father's birthday. When it was finished she booked passage aboard a cargo schooner out of Savannah, Georgia, bound for her home in

Washington. Pirates captured the vessel, blindfolded the crew and Theodosius, and then prodded them overboard. A skeleton crew was put aboard the captured vessel and taken in-tow. That night a storm struck, breaking the towline between the two ships, and the captured vessel ship drifted ashore near Cape Lookout. The pirates were afraid they would be caught if they went ashore, so they didn't try to retrieve their bounty.

Delia thought about her own experiences since she left home, how the shipwrecks were so commonplace in the area, and how survival under such primitive conditions was a major preoccupation among the people. She understood because her own life since she left London had been so completely focused on survival.

The winter months passed into warm early spring days. Curlew birds were nesting. Huge flocks of geese headed north in an undulating pattern along the horizon. The oleanders and crepe myrtles were blooming. Delia loved the sweet aroma of the wild honeysuckle, and gardenias, called graveyard flowers by the islanders, grew wild everywhere.

Delia was up early one warm morning in April, still in her nightclothes, preparing a breakfast of oatmeal and scratch biscuits, which would be used to sop blackstrap molasses. Suddenly the kitchen door flew open. There stood Percy, carrying a bag of something in his hand.

"My God, man!" said Delia. "Have you ever heard of knocking before entering?"

"Well, Red," he laughed, "eyeballing you, I had rather enter than knock." Seeing Miss Lucy standing in the doorway, he said, "Good morning, Miss Lucy. I jest come to ask Red if'n she would like to go feeling for flounders when the tide makes low today."

"Percy, you horny toad," said Miss Lucy. "Why don't ye leave the chile alone? Stop pestering her—and what is in that bag?"

"I bring you two curlews for yer supper," said Percy.

"Well, thanks, leave the birds and gets."

After he left, Delia asked, "What in the world did he mean, feeling for flounders? Sounds interesting."

"That's an old Indian way of catching flounders," said Miss Lucy. "Ye must wait until the tide is full ebb and the water in the small sloughs and estuaries is low and hot, making a flounder numb and sluggish. Ye very gently run yer hand along the bottom, and slowly crawl along until ye feel a flounder; it will be flat and slimy. Ye gently feel for its head and gig it with a sharp pointed stick or gig. If'n he is over a tenpounder, all hell breaks loose. Ye can't see fer the mud mixed with blood flying in all directions while you hang on for dear life. The last time I gigged one it took an hour to clean the mess out of my nose, ears and hair."

Hearing what Miss Lucy had to say about floundering, Delia had her doubts about trying it.

The fishy-tasting bird Percy had brought them for dinner was a wild curlew. It was two feet long with a long bill that curved downward. According to Miss Lucy, it was the only shorebird that nested on the island year-round. The islanders also ate the eggs, always leaving two in the nest so they wouldn't deplete the population.

Delia stopped eating curlew as she listened to Miss Lucy tell the story of Roy Duncan's accident. Delia had seen Roy carving a wooden curlew one day and wondered what happened to his face.

Miss Lucy explained, "When Roy was a young boy, he, his mother and father were walking along the shore one Sunday, looking for a curlew bird for their dinner.

"Roy ran ahead and stopped to examine an odd-looking shell. He called his father to come see his find. Carrying the cocked gun across his arm, he bent over Roy to see the shell and the gun accidentally fired, hitting the boy in the face."

"How awful, Miss Lucy. It's a wonder Roy survived," Delia grimaced.

Miss Lucy leaned forward, spit a stream of snuff spittle into the fireplace, straightened her apron and continued. "Yes, it is. With blood gushing down his face, he ran around the shore. His father, thinking he had shot his son's face off, ran after him. It is the custom on the island to kill the seriously wounded if thar is no hope for their survival."

"Oh my God, how barbaric," Delia said with a frown.

"No chile, it's done to relieve their suffering if they are mangled or bleeding to death, since the nearest doctor is three-and-a-half hours away by boat, and another hour on horseback. Roy made it to his Aunt Rose Owen's house. She washed the blood from his face and was holding him in her lap with a wet cloth pressed to his face, when his father rushed in. "'You don't have to kill him,' said Aunt Rose. 'He jest lost his nose and we can save him.'

"Now his face resembles a sea turtle—whar his nose should be thar are two holes slightly below his eyes."

Delia lay in bed that night and thought about the story of Roy Duncan. She had never heard of people dealing with tragedy in such a way, but could not help having a certain admiration for some of the islanders' customs. Their resignation to the limits facing them in responding to life-threatening catastrophes was understandable, but their solutions based on such resignation could at times be shocking. It was ironic how Roy Duncan now spent most of his time woodcarving, with a penknife, the same bird that was instrumental in his accident. He occasionally sold a few of his carvings on the mainland.

CHAPTER SIX

Delia was stoking the kitchen stove one spring morning when Miss Lucy appeared at the door. "I almost forgot," she said. "Tonight is the full moon in June when the turtles come ashore and lay. It's a big time on the island. We have a cookout on the beach, hunt for turtle eggs and sometimes we even have a broomstick marriage."

"What in the world is a broomstick marriage?" Delia asked.

"Well, if a preacher ain't around and a couple is itching to get married or pregnant, Percy, the self-appointed constable, performs the ceremony. The couple is required to jump a broomstick backwards. Two forked tree limbs are driven into the sand and a stick placed between them. They hold hands and jump the stick backwards. If they clear the stick, they are married. If they knock the stick down, they have to wait until the next full moon."

Late that afternoon everyone that was able assembled on the beach, where several men had started a fire beneath a big cast iron washpot filled with hog lard for frying fish. Sweet potatoes and sundried mullet roe were placed close to the fire for roasting. Hot coals were taken from the fire and placed underneath two three-leg skillets for frying lace cornbread. Delia and Miss Lucy furnished yaupon tea, flavored with sassafras oil from the aromatic bark of a sassafras tree.

While waiting for the moon to rise, the mood was greatly enhanced by the traditional sand-kicking hoedown, accompanied by guitar and tub-thumping. Accustomed to ballroom dancing, Delia thought this dance a little barbaric. Occasionally men would slip away from their wives and disappear behind a sand dune for a swig of corn liquor. Miss Lucy watched what was going on and had the privilege of being the only person on the beach with a chair.

The balmy gray twilight gradually faded as the moon rose in a silvery path across the ocean. It was a night made for beach parties, turtle egg hunting, and lovers. After their fill of food, people divided up in small groups for the egg hunt.

"How many eggs does a turtle normally lay?" Delia asked a lady standing near her with a bucket in her hand.

"Well, honey, they lays anywhere from a hundred to two hundred. After we takes about ten or twenty from her nest, we cover the sand back jest like she left it."

Delia helped look for turtle tracks, trying to find where they returned to the ocean from their nest near the edge of the sand dunes. This hunting continued until they gathered all they could use. The natives swore to the rich taste of the eggs and considered them quite a delicacy. For a week they would eat them boiled, fried, scrambled, or cooked in cakes.

Delia was appalled when she saw small children scrape barnacles from the back of a turtle after she laid and take turns riding her back to the water's edge. It didn't seem to bother the turtle; she crawled along at the same pace with or without a rider.

Holding hands, courting couples slipped away from the crowd. Delia couldn't help being envious, thinking of her beau, Ralph, left in London, and how their love was cut short by her abduction. Her moment of melancholy was suddenly interrupted when Percy put his arm around her waist.

"Come, Red. I'll show you all about turtle hunting, and you ain't lived until you've walked down a beach with me on a full moon in June."

"I'll walk a short way with you, Percy Tyndall. But, if you lay a hand on me, I'll cause you to gum your food and drink through a straw the rest of your life. And what in the hell are you planning to do with that old tub?"

"Yer trying to talk tough like ol' Queenie, ain't you?"

"Who is ol' Queenie?"

"That's what we all calls Miss Lucy, behind her back. Don't ye dare tell her I said so or she'll momick me for sure. The tub is to put crabs in. They like this here full moon same as turtles. But it ain't nothing like the year of the crab."

"All right smarty pants, what's the year of the crab?"

"Well, every seventeen years, like the locust, crabs by the hundreds wash ashore in the waves, most of them she crabs full of eggs. Then they rush back into the ocean. Running from the males," he laughed, "jest like yer doing. But they want to be caught."

Delia enjoyed walking on the edge of the surf, chasing crabs, and watching those she missed crawl quickly back into the sea. When they had the tub full of the largest crabs she had ever seen, she left Percy and went home, taking the catch with her.

The next day Delia watched Miss Lucy take the shells off the crabs and remove their guts. She made a stew of crabs, onions, potatoes, and salt pork. Cornmeal dumplings were added during the last fifteen minutes.

"You break the crab in two," she said, "and what you can't pick out, you suck out. Then you pour the pot licker over the pot dodger. When the gravy begins to drip off yer elbow, you are getting with it."

It was a hot, sultry day in the middle of August. Miss Lucy and Delia were facing the water in the shade of a large oak tree, trying to stay cool with the help of two cardboard fans.

Delia began to read the writing on the fan she was using. One side of the fan advertised Dick Cannon's Funeral Home, and featured a picture of a man in a coffin and a verse that read, "As you are so once was I, as I am, you soon shall be, so prepare yerself to follow me." The other side read, "Now is the time to get right with your Lord." Across the bottom was, "Our caskets are lined and waterproof. Group discount."

Delia laughed when she finished reading and knew by the smile on Miss Lucy's face and the twinkle in her eyes that she was about to launch into one of the sidesplitting stories she was famous for.

"These fans were brought to the island by a preacher. He asked that after his sermon the fans be put back on the pews whar he placed them. He said that the devil would take the soul of whoever walked out with one. He was another one of them long-winded preachers. By the time he wound down, everyone's rear end was numb from sitting on those hard benches, and all the fans did was stir up body odor. The church smelled like a billy goat pen."

She stopped to swat her fan at a wasp buzzing around her head. "When the preacher bowed his head and closed his eyes for his last long prayer, most of the fans were thrown out the window to be retrieved later. Those that didn't throw their fans out could read well enough to skeer the p'licker out of them."

Delia laughed so hard she had difficulty catching her breath. This was all the encouragement Miss Lucy needed.

"I'm here to tell you, chile, the last time thar was an August this hot we had one of the worst blows in twenty-five years. It hit on high tide, causing Silver Lake to rise eight feet above sea level. After the eye passed, the storm came around again. It blew a ten-foot tidal wave out of Silver Lake and almost swamped the whole island. My house had a foot of water inside and damage to the roof, but not as bad as some. Two weeks before the big blow, Beulia Guthrie's husband died and was buried in the front yard. The sand hadn't settled around his casket and the water washed it out of the ground through the front door, down the hall, and out the back door."

Her story was interrupted when the raccoon jumped into her lap. She settled him down and began to fan him.

"Oh God," Delia said, "I hope we don't have such a storm."

"It don't end thar," Miss Lucy said, spitting snuff spittle. "When the casket passed down the hallway, Beulia grabbed hold of one of its rope handles, climbed on top of the casket, and rode it into the sound, holding on for dear life. Good thing, for that po' woman can't swim a lick. That homemade casket of heart pine covered with pitch could have carried her to Bermuda.

"The next day they found her sitting on top of the casket, tangled in limbs of a large tree that had fallen in the water. She was ranting and raving, saying, 'Oh Lord, if'n I ever needed ye I needs ye now, and for Gaud's sake, don't send yer son 'cause this ain't no time for youngerns.' They had to hogtie her to get her down—she had gone completely loony."

Miss Lucy interrupted Delia's laughter, "What in the hell is that funny looking craft trying to maneuver through the mouth of the lake?"

"I don't know. Wonder where it's from," said Delia, rising from her chair.

Several men on the shore also saw the unusual looking craft and stopped their net mending, painting, or whittling and headed for the dock. "Whatever it is," Delia heard one say, "she'll go aground. The tide is mean low."

Finding the narrow channel, the craft slowly entered and anchored in the middle of Silver Lake.

"I ain't ever seed a scow like that," one of the men on the dock said. "She must belong to a Yankee, and what the hell is she doing coming in here? I'll bet ya'll a chew of tobacco it's one of them thar carpetbaggers."

"My Gaud, boys," Percy said, "she is squared off at both ends, and looks to be fifty feet long. Wonder how much water she draws? Will you look at that fancy carving around the top of her cabin? Reminds me of Sally's Sunday go-to-meeting drawers."

They sat in awe, watching a dory being lowered over the side of the craft and two men rowing toward the dock. "Good afternoon," the older man said when they arrived. Stepping from the dory he continued, "My name is Bill Sutton and this is my boatswain, Rip Harrison. We are in need of a motor mechanic for my houseboat. The engine started giving us trouble several miles out of New Bern. We just made it here and we can't go any farther."

"Yup, like I said," said Walter, "with that lingo he is a full-fledged Yankee." They all turned on their heels and walked off the dock, except Percy.

Delia and Miss Lucy, from the shade of the tree, observed all the excitement, and knew Percy stayed only for monetary reasons.

"We better go to that man's rescue before Percy skins him alive," said Miss Lucy.

They walked up behind Percy just as he said, "Yes sir, you can hire my mechanic—but I have to have ten dollars upfront money, like now."

"Percy, shut yer lying mouth, ye don't have any more of a mechanic than I do. Mister, the only person that works on motors around here is at the lighthouse, yonder on that point," Miss Lucy said, pointing toward the south. "It would be shorter for you to row over in that little contraption than to walk around the shore."

They were pulling away from the dock when Miss Lucy hollered, "When ya'll return, come by my house fer a drink of cool."

"Should you ask those men by the house?" Delia asked. "We don't know anything about them. Did you see Mr. Sutton's left hand? His little finger is drawn back toward his wrist."

"Yes, I did, and it's a shame. He seems like sech a nice man . . . purty too," Miss Lucy said, smiling.

Late that afternoon both men accepted Miss Lucy's invitation and were served yaupon tea, which they quickly substituted for a glass of water. Bill explained why he came south and how they arrived on Conch Island.

He told them his home was Mount Kisco, New York. When he was twenty and a student at Harvard he had his first arthritis attack, and his condition gradually became worse. During that time he became engaged to Helen Craft, his high school sweetheart.

Rip interrupted to ask Miss Lucy if he could use her facilities.

"If'n ye means what I thinks ye means, it's out back of the garden."

"You can go out the back door, Mr. Harrison," said Delia. "Come, I'll show you."

When she returned, Bill continued with his story. "A week before the wedding Helen was found dead in bed of a heart attack. Devastated, I drank heavily, and with the progressive illness of arthritis, my hand began to draw. My doctor told me I had to leave the cold Northern winters and seek a warmer climate.

"I hired Rip as my boatswain and nurse; he had some medical training and worked for a while in a New York hospital."

Bill paused and asked Delia for a glass of water. She returned with the water and, thinking Bill was through with his story, asked, "Did you find a mechanic?"

"Yes, I did, but some motor parts have to be ordered from Norfolk. After I passed a few dollars, one of the lifesaving station men considered it an emergency and sent a message for the parts to be delivered by the mail boat in two weeks."

Bill noticed Delia's accent was different from Miss Lucy's and the men on the docks and asked, "Miss Delia, may I ask where are you from?"

Must I tell my life story again? she thought. "I was born in England and came to this country several years ago. While here on a visit, I fell in love with the island and its people, so I decided to stay a while."

Delia winked at Miss Lucy, who put her hand to her mouth to stifle a smile.

Waiting for the motor parts from New Bern, Delia and Bill Sutton became good friends and often fished from the stern of the houseboat. This activity was only occasionally successful, but they didn't seem to mind. The real attraction was watching the porpoises darting and jumping around the boat. Since this occurred several times when Bill and Delia came aboard, they expected these graceful mammals to be waiting to show off and entertain them. Of course, on these performing days there were no fish around to be caught. On the days they were successful, Rip made delectable dishes and sent Miss

Lucy a plate of whatever was left. She would reciprocate by sending him her "straight up and down Southern cooking" or "gut-ripping hot stew," as she called her victuals.

Bill and Delia's walks around the island became a familiar sight to the natives. They were often seen observing the flora, gathering seashells left high on the sandy beach, or retrieving them from the receding surf. Skeleton hulls of shipwrecks, buried in the sand, became raw material for competitive storytelling, each one designed to outdo the other.

Three weeks later Bill received a letter from the Norfolk shipyard. The letter explained that the parts for his motor had to be shipped from Baltimore and would arrive in six weeks.

Rip and Percy were disappointed when they heard the news, but Delia was glad to see it didn't phase Bill. She was delighted the islanders liked Bill and Rip, and thought it unusual considering the brief time they had been there. Of course, Delia's advice on how to get along with the islanders helped the two Northerners establish good relationships.

One night in early September, Bill and Delia were wading in the surf, kicking up tiny sparkles of phosphorescence in the water. *Like millions of fireflies,* thought Delia. Suddenly an orange glow appeared on the horizon, momentarily giving the island a golden hue, before the full moon appeared. Its brightness gradually extinguished the stars and the Milky Way as it progressively ascended.

"I have never seen the moon so large or beautiful," Bill said. "Look, my dear, the man in the moon is smiling at us." He put his arm around her. She turned from watching the moon and faced him. Their eyes met, the distance between them gradually closed, and they kissed a tentative, gentle kiss that lingered on.

Bill spoke first, saying, "I have wanted to do that ever since I first saw you. I have fallen in love with you and hope you love me enough to marry me."

"Oh Bill, I love you too," she said. Then she paused. "But you know very little about me. I need more time before I will be free to divulge all my life experiences. For now let's agree to be good friends."

Delia thought she had embarrassed Bill when he didn't say anything for a while. She suspected he thought he had prematurely exposed his inner feelings. Then Bill said, "I think you are right, we do need more time together, and I'm just happy we have these moments with each other." With that, they embraced and kissed again. It was an evening Delia wanted to hang on to forever.

Through all of this, Percy hid behind a tree, observing everything, especially the silhouette of them kissing. He had followed them from as far back as the village. Rushing back to the store where the men gathered every evening after supper to whittle, chew tobacco, and swap tales of the sea, Percy staggered in almost breathless. "Boys, I jest now catched that Yankee tapping Delia!"

The men laughed. "I'll swear I never seed the likes of him," Zeke said. "He wants to tap her hisself. Ye best shut yer mouth, if'n ye know what's good fer ye. Miss Lucy will momick ye fer sure, if'n she gets wind of that lie ye jest tol'." Laughing, he added, "But that full moon, she could make ye love a fence post—even yer mother-in-law."

Delia returned home that evening and found Miss Lucy hemorrhaging periodically.

"One thing is for sho' honey, it damn well ain't a miscarriage. No one seen a star in the east, have they?" Miss Lucy said.

"I'll go get Rip, since he is the only one we know with some sort of medical training," Delia said and hurried out the door.

Rip arrived and told Miss Lucy she would have to remove all her clothes for an examination.

"My bloomers too?" she asked.

"I'm afraid so, Miss Lucy. I have to see why you are hemorrhaging."

"Ye mean to tell me ye are going to see my Cootzee May? Hell no, I'm not taking my bloomers off fer ye or no damn body. I've never completely disrobed in my whole life and I ain't going to start now."

Bill Sutton arranged for the lifesaving longboat to take Miss Lucy and Delia to a doctor in New Bern.

Miss Lucy cussed a blue streak the whole time the nurse prepared her for the examination. As Delia left the room she heard her say, "Youngerns, I'm being momicked this day."

Thirty minutes later, Dr. Maxwell gave Delia the prognosis. "She has a cyst on her cervix as large as an orange. I'm afraid it's malignant and I need to perform a complete hysterectomy. It should be removed as soon as possible. I think its best if you tell her—I won't," he said, laughing. "That woman can outcuss a Norfolk sailor. She called me 'Old Sawbones' and the nurse 'Big Nose,' and said that if she had that nose full o' nickles she could buy a three-mast schooner."

When Delia relayed Dr. Maxwell's message to Miss Lucy, all hell broke loose. "Ain't no Sawbones going to cut on this here body," she said. "He probably uses a fish skinner for a knife. Give me my drawers and let's get the hell out of here."

Delia finally persuaded Miss Lucy to have the operation by telling her how much she would be missed on the island and that Percy would run everyone loony and pester her until she would have to leave.

"If that horny bastard lays a hand on ye, I'll kick his arse so raw, he'll have to stand a month. Tell Old Sawbones I'm ready and to be sure that fish skinner is sharp and be damn sho' I'm good an' sleep before he starts cutting."

Delia had just reached the door when Miss Lucy called her back. "I needs to make my will, jest in case Sawbones cuts me slam to the hollow. Gets that nurse with a stern as wide as two ax handles to come in here for a witness, and tell her not to get too close. Her breath smells like week-old collard pot licker."

She willed Delia her house on the island and what little money she had in the New Bern Bank.

Delia sat alone in the small waiting room while Miss Lucy was in surgery. Teary-eyed, she stared out a window that faced the Trent River, thinking what would happen to her if Miss Lucy died. She thought how kind she had been to her and how much she loved her. She would miss the colorful, rough way she described everything and everybody, but at the same time showing compassion for others.

Two hours later, Delia was standing by Miss Lucy, holding her hand, when she became conscious.

"Well chile, I guess I made it. Give me my clothes and let's get the hell out of here and head for the island."

"Miss Lucy, you can't go now, you must have patience," said Delia, "and patience is not one of your virtues." Delia couldn't believe she was giving Miss Lucy orders.

On the fifth day, Miss Lucy was dressed and ready to leave when Dr. Maxwell walked into her room. "It's your doctor, in case you don't recognize me without my white coat. Here's your fish knife," he said, smiling, handing her a surgeon's knife. "I want you to have it in remembrance of Old Sawbones and your operation."

"Thanks, Sawbones," she said. "It looks like a flounder skinner to me. How many did ye skin before ye used it on me?"

"Without a doubt, you are the most ornery, cantankerous patient I've ever had. But I've enjoyed every minute of your stay," he said, laughing. "And by the way, a Mr. Bill Sutton took care of your hospital bill."

"Instead of paying, I was going to charge you for cutting me from stem to stern. Cootzee May will never be the same. But if ye are ever on the island, come to see me for a mess of pluck and mullet roe."

"What in the world is pluck?" Dr. Maxwell asked.

"Come Miss Lucy, the boat is waiting for us," Delia said, smiling, She didn't know what Miss Lucy would say or do next.

"My Gaud, man," Miss Lucy continued. "How could ye be so smart and never have eaten pluck? Ye haven't lived 'til ye have had a belly full. It's the gizzard and liver from the mullet, and I'll bet ye don't even know the mullet is the only fish with a gizzard like a chicken."

He shook his head and said, "No I didn't."

"Well now, Sawbones, ye have a new wrinkle in yer brain."

Dr. Maxwell saw Delia and Miss Lucy off on the boat and promised to see them in the fall, when the mullets ran south and he could try Miss Lucy's pluck.

Three hours later the boat turned to enter the mouth of Silver Lake, and a mournful sound came across the water.

"What's that weird sound?" Delia asked.

"Oh, that's ol' Zeke blowing his conch shell," Miss Lucy said. "It's a strict rule that he blow the conch only in an emergency or if something unusual is about to happen. Two short blasts if someone dies, is killed, or if a hurricane is brewing. One long blast, like now, for a special occasion. Must be that

I'm coming home alive, not feet first. It's an honor to be blasted ashore. Ol' Zeke is the last one living that knows how to blow the conch."

"Who started such an unusual practice? Sounds like you, Miss Lucy," said Delia.

"No, it started with the Weetock Indians. It was blown to warn folks of approaching danger."

"Whatever happened to the Weetock Indians?" Delia asked.

"Many years ago the Indians were the only people on the island. One day a pirate ship put ashore two sailors with syphilis. The story goes that several squaws caught the disease from the sailors and passed it around. Thar were but very few left when the first settlers arrived. They taught them the art of blowing the conch, which has been handed down for generations."

A crowd gathered on the dock to welcome Miss Lucy. After the boat was securely tied, Percy reached out his hand to help her onto the dock.

"What did they do to you, Miss Lucy?" he asked.

Noticing his left hand was bandaged, she said, "Ye ol' rapscallion. What trouble did ye get into while I was gone? And if'n ye must know, they removed my damn flues. It's what they should have done to ye years ago. I feel hollow as a gourd!"

"Miss Lucy, how ye do carry on. Ain't nobody going to momick my manhood. And as fer this hand, I cut it while nubbing coon oysters fer ye and Delia."

"Well, thanks Percy, but the last oysters ye gave me were the size of kitten tongues. And, besides, they gave me the backdoor trots."

On the day before Thanksgiving, the mail boat brought the spare parts for Bill's houseboat and a turkey he had ordered a month earlier from New Bern. He invited Miss Lucy and Delia to share Thanksgiving Day with him and Rip aboard his boat.

Miss Lucy, reluctant to ride in the two-man dinghy out to the houseboat anchored in the middle of Silver Lake, said, "Gaud a'mighty! Bill Sutton, if'n ye think I'm riding in that thing yer one addled Yankee. I had a scab on my behind larger than that thing." Bill hired the lifesaving boat to transport her over, and later, bring her back to shore.

Several times during the day, Delia saw Bill reading the barometer. "Is there going to be a change in the weather?" she asked.

"I don't know, but the barometer has been steadily falling since noon. There might be a storm. We better get Miss Lucy ashore."

Delia found Miss Lucy in a recliner on the aft deck, drinking the third mint julep Bill had mixed for her.

"This is some fancy Southern drink," she said, taking a sip. "I ain't ever had it before, but it's some kinda good." Rising from the recliner, she had to be helped by Delia.

"Why Miss Lucy, I do believe you're tipsy."

"Tipsy! Chile, I'm high as a Georgia pine. Now I know why those high and mighty, corset-stuffed women that call themselves Southern belles bat their eyelashes at the menfolk, look cross-eyed, and giggle silly. I'm here to tell ye this here stuff is potent. I believe it's better'n asafetida fer what ails ye."

Bill told Miss Lucy there might be a storm and he was taking her ashore.

"I didn't tell ye what I've been 'specting, cause I didn't want to spoil yer day. The air is too calm and clammy. I've been watching gulls and pelicans, a few at a time, leave the island fer the mainland. They know when a storm is brewing."

Delia thought about the story of the hurricane that carried Beulia out of the house on her husband's casket, and was worried something horrible might happen again.

"Look at the cloud scuds banking in the south," said Miss Lucy. "It'll strike about midnight, blowing a poppy cot and meaner'n a wet setting hen. We must go ashore and have Old Zeke blow the conch horn in case folks ain't noticed the birds leaving the island or seen the dark clouds scudding. If'n I were ye, Bill, I'd take this here floating house and anchor her both bow and stern on the leeward side of the island."

"Thanks, Miss Lucy, I'll do that," he said.

On the way to the dock Miss Lucy called their attention to the hurricane flag being raised on top of the lighthouse.

Early in the night Delia saw flashes of lightning followed by thunder from the south. A short time later, gale winds began to cool the island. Around midnight the wind intensified, just as Miss Lucy predicted. Billowing waves pounded the beach relentlessly as the storm turned into a full hurricane. The house shook, windows creaked, and doors rattled from flaws of the howling wind.

This was an unusual experience for Delia. "Oh God! Miss Lucy," she cried, "we are going to be blown away!"

"Chile, I've seen worse storms than this," Miss Lucy said, trying to soothe her. "Bring a cheer and sit here in the middle of the room with Sooner and me. In case a window blows, you don't want to get cut with the flying glass. And stop pacing the floor, you've purty near wore it out."

Delia sat curled up in a chair next to Miss Lucy, shivering, while the wind gusted for about an hour. Then a dead calm set in.

"Thank God it's over," said Delia, starting toward the kitchen.

"Come back, chile, it's jest the eye of the storm. In a few minutes it'll hit agin."

Dawn broke the next morning with a fair, cloudless sky and a calm sea. Delia and Miss Lucy were out inspecting the property for damages wrought during the night. Her privy, minus the brass chandelier, which Delia had removed the afternoon before, was on its side.

"When it comes to privies," said Miss Lucy, "hurricanes show no mercy." With the exception of a couple of missing roofs and skiffs, the extent of the damage this time was a few uprooted trees and debris piled up in people's yards. The islanders knew not to transfer their good fortune into a state of lethargy toward future storms. They never took storms for granted because they might not be so lucky the next time one hit, and there would be a next time.

Bill Sutton and Rip weren't so fortunate. During the storm the wind spun the boat around several times, breaking the bowline loose and washing the vessel halfway on shore. Rip received a slight concussion and a broken arm when he was thrown up against the bulkhead.

After Delia saw Miss Lucy's roof was intact and the only real damage was to the privy, she rushed down the shoreline to see how Bill and Rip had fared. She found Bill trying to put a splint on Rip's arm, with Rip giving the instructions.

"Oh Delia," Bill said, "I'm happy to see you are all right. Will you stay with Rip while I go hire someone from the life-saving station to carry him to the doctor in New Bern?"

Delia finished wrapping Rip's arm and helped him find his clothes, which were scattered among everything else onboard.

"Please pack them all," Rip said. "Bill can stay if he wants to, but I'm leaving for New Bern, then New York, as soon as I can find transportation. I've had enough hurricanes to last me the rest of my life. Bill's health has improved tremendously since we have been here. Guess this crude isolated island agrees with him. He really doesn't need me anymore. He can find a boatswain on one of these islands. All he needs now is a pilot and a maid, because he knows nothing about domestic work."

The longboat was pulling away from the shore when Bill yelled to Delia, "Ask Miss Lucy if I may board with her until my houseboat can be repaired. I will pay her well. See you in a few days."

Delia relayed the message to Miss Lucy, and she agreed, saying, "That's one Yankee I like. He can stay as long as he likes."

Over Miss Lucy's objections, Delia gave up her room for their boarder. She spent the next day cleaning out her few belongings, and transformed a small storage shed connected to the kitchen into a bedroom.

"All I have to say, chile, is ye must think a lot of Sutton—not that I blame you. If'n I could call back about forty years, he could put his shoes under my bed any ol' time."

The second day after the storm, Delia awoke to the sound of the conch horn. From the front door she saw people running toward the ocean side of the island. *What in the world is all the excitement about?* she thought. She called Miss Lucy to go with her to see what the commotion was.

A four-mast schooner was about to founder on the beach. *It is hard to believe she managed to slip through the Diamond Shoals barrier,* thought Delia. The schooner floated free in the deep lagoon between the beach and shoal. Her unfurled sails were tattered, but her hull seemed to be intact. She was evidently without a helmsman, however, as she appeared out of control by her zigzag movements. From the beach they could see no one aboard.

66

Percy and several men launched a skiff and rowed out to the vessel. "Ship ahoy, is anyone aboard?" yelled one of the men. After several calls, no answer was received, so they climbed to the deck with the use of a rope hanging over the port side. It was like a ghost ship. The only sounds were the creaking of the rigging, the slow rolling of a loose barrel of molasses, and a cat's weak meow coming from the captain's quarters.

"Who in the hell would sail on a ship with a black cat aboard?" Walter said. "It's same as having a woman aboard, and both would jinx a dinghy. No wonder she ran into trouble."

The men found the decks were scrubbed clean. The table in the mess hall was laid with a set of dinnerware. Even the clock, which Percy later took, was hanging on the bulkhead in the captain's quarters, still ticking. They searched every nook and cranny where a person could be hiding—in the forecastle, in the captain's cabin, and in the crew's living quarters where they found clothes hanging neatly on pegs. All were a sign of a hasty departure.

The ship's log noted the last entry was made on Friday the 10th, 1889, and read as follows:

The *Emerald Sea* of Ireland. Last port Savannah, Georgia. Headed for Norfolk, Virginia, with a cargo of lumber. We are under full sail hoping to outrun a storm brewing on our stern. Latitude showing we are off the North Carolina coast. Striving to pass the dangerous Diamond Shoals before the storm overtakes us.
Capt. O'Conner

The men gathered up the hawsers neatly coiled about the deck and tied the ends of several around the bow cleats. Taking the hawsers and cat with them, they rowed back to the beach, swung her bow around so she would face the shore, and tied her to a large oak tree. Delia heard men say that with the taut ropes and floor tide at midnight, she'd be beached when the tide ebbed.

The next morning Delia saw the ship lying on her starboard side with three-fourths of her keel showing. *What a beautiful ship,* she thought, *with her bottom painted red, her gray hull and her white gunwales.* Fastened to her bowsprit was the full-length figure of a mermaid, which Percy later confiscated.

Miss Lucy walked up to several ladies standing near. "She looks so pitiful lying there with her bottom showing. I know just how she feels, and can even imagine I hear her whisper, 'Some jackass help me.'"

Delia learned that according to island law, handed down for generations, any crippled vessel that came ashore, manned or unmanned, became island property, and anyone wanting a share of the bounty had to help dismantle her. Ships were treated with the utmost respect. Before a ship was dismantled, she was decommissioned and homage was paid to her as if she had a soul.

By late evening everything of value inside the ship had been taken. The hull could wait. The pounding waves would break her up, making it easier to salvage the wooden planks, which would go toward patching houses and replacing privies that were damaged or destroyed during the hurricane.

Delia listened to all sorts of theories concerning the fate of the *Emerald Sea.* Some said that there might have been a mutiny and that perhaps the officers were killed, and then the crew left in the ship's dory and were lost during the storm. But Delia thought Buck Marine, an old seafaring man, had the most likely story.

"I tell ye youngerns, that ship went aground," he said as he pointed toward the ocean, "on that spit of sand shoal. The captain thought he had grounded her on the dangerous Diamond or Frying Pan Shoals. With the storm bearing down on her stern, he must have thought she would be driven further up on the shoal and broken up. He panicked and gave the order to abandon ship."

Delia anxiously waited for the man to finish filling his pipe and get on with his story.

"They should have stuck with her. She freed her keel when the first storm wave hit and rode the storm out into the lagoon. She is one tough ship. It would be something if the crew saw her pass by them before they capsized and drowned. We soon jest might find a few bodies floating on the surf or washed ashore. That is, if the sharks didn't get them first."

Before the *Emerald Sea* showed any signs of giving the sea the satisfaction of breaking up her hull, Bill and a marine investigator from Norfolk arrived on the mail boat. Owners of the ship had hired the investigator to find her whereabouts. It had been reported that she went aground somewhere in the vicinity of Conch Island with a cargo of teakwood. Of course, Delia knew the man would be told by all he encountered that there hadn't been a wreck on the island in several years. Soon after his arrival, the investigator happened to walk into Percy's store and saw the mermaid statue standing in the corner. He knew it belonged to the missing ship, and said to Percy, "May I ask you, sir, where you acquired the mermaid?"

Miss Lucy said Percy could momick the truth with the straightest face, better than anyone she had ever seen, and that he would climb a tree to tell a lie rather than stand on the ground and tell the truth.

"Well, it goes like this," Percy said. "I came across this here man while out in the sound clamming yestiddy. He had this thang aboard his skiff, said he was going to take it to the mainland and sell it. I made him a good offer and he took me up on it, and thar she is. Now if ye want, she is yern fer fifty bucks."

"No, I don't think so," the man said.

"How about twenty-five then? I paid more fer it than that."

"No, just tell me where I can find the fellow who sold you the mermaid."

"How the hell do I know? He don't live on this island," said Percy. "He was jest a po' man out clamming fer his living. And I think ye oughtta take the mail boat back to the mainland. She leaves in thirty minutes flat."

"I shall seek information on the other islands, and try to find the man who sold you the mermaid. I have legal authorization from the marine headquarters and the ship's owners to claim the boat and her cargo."

The mail boat, with the investigator aboard, had hardly cleared the dock before Percy hastily called several men to the store. "Ye know the man that highfalutin' Bill Sutton came back to the island with? He acted snottier'n a banks' ram. Tol' me he was going to come back and claim our wreck. He thinks he's sharper'n rat droppings, but we'll outsmart him. Get everybody, even yer womenfolk and youngerns, to the beach. We must take the rest of the ship today!"

Delia was helping Bill settle into his room when all of the sudden they heard the sound of planks being ripped, the pounding of hammers, and men hollering.

"My Gaud," said Miss Lucy from her rocking chair. "'Pears like they are finishing off the *Emerald Sea*. I can't remember hearing the men work so hard or fast. Usually they are slower'n 'lasses on a cold day. Something is in the wind and I'll bet Percy is behind it. Come Delia, Bill—let's see what's going on."

From the top of a dune the people below resembled ants working in a frenzy around a mound. Bill was excited when he saw that a pile of lumber stacked on the beach was teakwood.

"Delia, that must be the lumber the shipbuilders in Norfolk are expecting," said Bill. "They were out of teak, and looking for a ship to arrive from Trinidad. They will contact me when it arrives."

Percy was standing close by and tried to look busy, but he was listening to Bill and Delia's conversation. Several minutes later, he approached Bill. "That's my lumber. I toted it outta her hull meself, but I'll sell it to ye right cheap."

"How much?" Bill asked.

"Well, let's see. How about fifty dollars and you haul it away today?"

"I'll give twenty-five and you move it for me."

"When do I get my money?"

"When you deliver the lumber. I must find a place to store it first."

"You better hurry 'cause I ain't got time to putter all day."

Bill and Delia laughed when they heard Percy mutter as he walked away, "That man is tighter'n a tick. Bet he'd skin a flea fer it's taller."

Late that evening the lumber was safely stored in an old abandoned shack Bill found on the edge of the village. Percy paid several men twenty cents each to move it.

Bill started to pay by check when Percy stopped him. "Man, yer crazier than a loon. What do ye think I'm going to do with that piece of paper, put it in my privy? I want that green stuff. Last time I seed one of them banks was in New Bern and that was six years ago."

"The reason he'll not go to New Bern," Miss Lucy said, laughing, "is that he was run out of town by the high sheriff 'cause he sold the sheriff's wife a big fat wharf rat fer a squir-rel. When the po' woman heard what she had eaten, she almost upchucked her toenails."

"Why do you momick me," said Percy, "when you tol' me you were glad I did, and that she acted stuck up jest cause her old man was sheriff? 'Sides, that woman is uglier than a blow-fish."

Late that afternoon all that was left of the *Emerald Sea* were staves and keel. *Soon the tidal waves and wind will drive her further ashore,* thought Delia, *where the shifting sands will bury her. Years later her bleached, silver-gray skeleton, pock-marked with dead barnacles, will be exposed. She will be indis-tinguishable from the many wrecks that preceded her.*

News spread fast throughout the island that the marine investigator was run off of Portsmouth Island and left for Norfolk in a hurry when he asked about the shipwreck. Delia could have told him the islanders were too close-knit to tell on each other, and the money he would be paid wasn't worth risk-ing his life for.

Through the few years Delia had been on the island, she learned that all the folks were close friends or blood relatives, and names established during the first settlement were still prominent generations later. They saw their lives as being calm, peaceful, and for the most part uneventful, except for an occasional storm, which they seemed to take in stride. They often used the expression, "What is to be, sho'ly will be."

Shortly after the marine investigator left, salvaged items from the *Emerald Sea* began to appear all over the island. Pots, dishes and other kitchen utensils from the ship's galley were particularly noticeable. Planks were used to build new skiffs and privies, and to patch houses. In some cases the privies were enlarged to incorporate two holes, like Miss Lucy's. Until then Miss Lucy had been very proud that hers was they only two-hole privy on the island. When other two-holes began to appear, she said, "Well by Gaud, I'll make mine a three-holer, with a small one fer the youngerns."

"I'll give you some of my teakwood," Bill said. "I have more than I need, and then you will have the most expensive three-holer on all the islands."

"Bill, you will make me prouder'n a peacock with two tails. Delia, will you please see Robert O'Neal fer me? I want him to start right away, and tell him I want a small porthole on the door instead of a half moon like everybody else. And it must be painted whiter'n a hant."

After Miss Lucy's privy was finished, Bill hired Robert O'Neal to build a new deck and refurbish the inside of his houseboat. A mechanic from the lighthouse was hired to repair the engine.

Robert O'Neal was quite a storyteller. While working on Bill's boat, he kept Delia and Bill amused with tales his father and grandfather told him while growing up on the island. He claimed they all were based on truth, even though some were hard to believe.

One day he asked Delia and Bill whether Miss Lucy had told them about Teaches Light.

"No, but I know you will tell us," said Delia. "What's Teaches Light?"

"Well, it's this here light that sometimes appears on dark nights, to the nor'eastern side of the island. It sways back and forth, about ten feet above the ground." He went on to say his grandpa told him that Blackbeard buried his treasure there. "Inside of the wooden cask is supposed to be the head of one of his pirates 'cause he caught him in the forecastle tapping his lady friend. You can't get an islander to go near that haunted light. They say that pirate is still looking fer his head."

Two months passed and Robert O'Neal had worked very little on the houseboat. Bill complained to Delia and Miss Lucy one evening about the work habits of the men on the island. "I am amazed that they will stop whatever they are doing, drop their tools right where they are working and walk off, sometimes for the rest of the day. Then some days they don't show up at all."

"That's the way they are," Miss Lucy said. "They've been slower'n molasses fer generations and they ain't gonna' change."

"This morning Robert said he was going clam signing. What in the world is clam signing?" Bill asked.

"Well, I'll tell ye," said Miss Lucy. "This came from the Weetock Indians. When a clam feeds it leaves a small hole in the sand or mud in the shape of a keyhole. On low tide we search around sand shoals and mud flats fer the sign. The clam is usually buried two or three inches deep. A whittled stick or knife is used to flip out the clam."

"Is that the only way the folks catch clams?" asked Bill.

"No, sometimes in the summer when clams are scarce, the islanders go out in the sound on five-foot stilts and use clam tongs. A float is tied to their waist fer support and to hold the clams."

"Miss Lucy," said Delia, "tell Bill the tale you told me about the couple that came through and stopped to clam."

"Well, some years ago, this highfalutin' couple came through on a small sailboat from outta state or Gaud-knows-whar. They saw several islanders standing knee deep in the sound, a good distance from shore, tonging fer clams. They dropped anchor near Walt Wayhab and one of the fur'ners said, 'Hello there fellow, can we clam here?'

"'Sure, go ahead if ye want to,' said Walt.

"Taking two large buckets, the couple jumped overboard and went out of sight, surfing. The man yelled, 'Help us, you fool! Why didn't you tell us the water is over our heads? And you're abnormal, anyone tall as you are.' Now, that fellow said the wrong thing.

"'Well, dingbat, ye got yerself in that mess so now ye can get yerself out. If'n I wanted to help ye, which I don't, these here stilts don't move around so easy,' said Walt. They managed to get out, left in a hurry, and Walt retrieved their sunken buckets."

Three months went by and the houseboat wasn't finished. Bill told Delia that he was going to fire O'Neal and hire someone from the mainland. Delia talked him out of it. "If you want to remain friends with the islanders and not be harassed until you have to leave, don't fire O'Neal. The people have begun to accept you; firing him and hiring someone from off the island tells them you don't trust one of their own. I'll ask Miss Lucy to light a fire under him, as she would say. If anyone can make him work faster, she will be the one to do so."

One morning Delia answered a knock at the door and there stood Zeke with a bag in his hands. "Tell Miss Lucy here is the fish she wanted," he said, "and if you would like to see a whale, thar is a dead one out here that beached herself last night. She's a big one. It'll be a while before we get rid of the stink. Been a spell since the last one washed ashore, and it stunk fer a month. See ye, Miss Delia." He turned and left before Delia could thank him.

Delia, Bill, and Miss Lucy headed for the beach side of the island to see the whale. Climbing the last sand dune, they saw her lying on her side in a foot of water. Her cavernous mouth was wide open, revealing yellow-tinged fuzz rather than teeth. Delia heard someone say it was for straining plankton, a baleen whale's main source of food. *Oh God,* Delia thought, *what a pitiful sight.* Small minnows darted in and out of her mouth and a few crabs nibbled at her tongue. A huge gash near her tail appeared recently cut. A number of seagulls were picking at the wound and several more awaited their turn. In the distance they could see more gulls approaching and heard their loud screeching long before their arrival. Bill estimated the whale was at least fifty feet long, and her side stood eight feet above the water's edge. The next ebb tide would leave her high and dry on the shore.

Standing in awe of the majestic mammal, Delia heard an old man, who evidently knew about whales, talking.

"By the looks of her milk glands, she was about to spawn. If she could've stayed at sea a little while longer she would've birthed that pup. And if my recollection is right, it would've been her last one, 'cause she is old." He went on to say, "I figure what happened is that during low tide last night she foundered on that first shoal." He pointed toward a sand shoal barely showing above the water. "Being heavy with pup and exhausted from flouncing around trying to free herself, a damn shark took a bite outta her. Must have been a big mako by the size of the cut and teeth marks. Guess with one last lunge she slipped into the lagoon, or that shark would've eaten much more of her."

The weather was warm and after a few days, when the wind blew in the right direction, the stench from the decomposed whale could be smelled as far north as Oregon Inlet and as far south as Portsmouth Island.

"The one thing about that Gaud-awful stink," said Miss Lucy, "is it makes my three-burner privy smell like Hout's cologne. It even gets in my food. Today my collards tasted like they were a month old."

After gulls and buzzards picked the skeleton clean, people begin to break away the vertebrae. Miss Lucy told Delia, "Ask Percy to bring me two vertebrae and I might pay him something."

"What do you want a whale vertebrae for, Miss Lucy?" Delia asked.

"I'll put it on my front piazza to hold my flowerpots. It's good luck to have a whale's backbone near the entrance to yer home. They look right purty after they bleach out white." She went on to say that whales' jawbones were flexible and were sold to make corset stays and other things.

Then Miss Lucy laughed and said someone told her that there was a rough tavern on the waterfront in Norfolk with a baleen whale's jaws for a doorway. "A man entered the tavern one day like when the whale swallowed Jonah, except Jonah was sober when he was upchucked."

It was the middle of May when the last deck board on the houseboat was nailed in place and her hull freshly painted. A launching was planned for the next day. Bill paid the lifesaving crew to tie the longboat to the stern and, with the help of the men on the island, the boat was pulled away from shore.

He invited the men who helped aboard for a cruise party. Reaching the sound channel, Bill broke out the booze he had ordered a month earlier for the occasion. Never having had that much store-bought liquor, they went into a drinking frenzy. After thirty minutes out in the sound, one of the men fell overboard. Bill rescued him, but then several men got into a drunken argument over who was the best pilot, so he decided to return to the island before someone was seriously injured or wrecked his houseboat. Just before sunset, he pulled up to the pier.

Some of the men were on the top deck singing and a few were dancing a jig. Standing on the dock waiting for them were their wives, Miss Lucy, and Delia.

"Uh oh, boys, those women look madder'n wet setting hens," said Luke. He then yelled to his wife, "Bless yer heart, me love, yer purtier than a speckled puppy. The devil made me do it, but I won't do it agin." He must've thought he sounded hen-pecked, since he added, "Woman, I don't want any lambasting out of you jest 'cause I'm all lickered up. Why don't you mosey on home and fix a mess of conch stew. I'm so hungry I could eat a bull and yell fer his horns."

Delia put her hand to her mouth to repress a laugh. "Luke Starns, you old fossil," said Miss Lucy, "these women have been worried half to death. Whar in the world have ya'll been? We all thought the boat sank and ya'll drowned, but I see thar is no sech luck. I tol' yer wives to lambaste the hell out of ye. I hope all ye get to eat fer two days is pot licker. Maybe two days of the backdoor trots will purge that booze out of yer guts." Turning on her heel, she and Delia walked off the dock.

CHAPTER SEVEN

The men took no offense; they knew Miss Lucy loved them and was just worried about their safety.

"I guess ol' Queenie tol' you a mouthful, Luke," said Walter.

"That goes fer ye too, Walter Wahab," said his wife Lula. Lula weighed about 250 pounds to Walter's 140. "Get on this here dock, I'm taking ye home and souse ye with a bucket of water. I'll make yer eyes look more like scaled hog asses than they do now. It'll be a week afore ye drink agin."

Luke bent over laughing. "Ye best do what she says, Walter. She can knock ye down by jest blowing her breath on ye. And if'n she sits down on ye, Gaud a'mighty, she'll mash you flatter'n a flounder!"

The women followed Lula, who had Walter by the ear, off the dock.

"I apologize for causing you men all this trouble," said Bill. "I should have returned to port sooner and served fewer drinks."

"Ah, don't ye worry none," said Luke. "We know how to handle our confounded women, don't we boys? Tonight we will lie and tell them how purty they are and how their skin is soft as a baby's behind. Then they'll become limber'n a dish rag and 'pear likeable."

A week later, Bill received a letter from Beaufort telling him the new furniture and fixtures for his houseboat had arrived, and they could be installed as soon as he brought the boat into town.

Finding a pilot to navigate the boat through the unmarked channels between Conch Island and Beaufort wasn't easy. Only a few had ever been that far. Finally, he found a man on Portsmouth Island named Fillmore Owens, who said, "I know every sand shoal betwixt Conch Island and Wilmington. I can leave in a week."

After Bill made several attempts to talk Delia into going with him to Beaufort, she said, "Bill, remember when I told you someday I would tell you about my life? Let's walk on the beach and I will tell you why I cannot go to Beaufort. No one on the island knows except Miss Lucy."

They walked a mile up the beach, and after she told Bill her story, Bill took her in his arms, and with tears said, "My dear, you know I love you. God, you have lived through hell. Please marry me so I can take care of you. I've inherited enough money for us to live well for the balance of our lives. After the boat is finished, I will come back for you."

Delia looked into his eyes and, smiling, put her head on his shoulder. "I love you too, Bill. You are the most compassionate and kind man I have ever met, and I will be happy to be your wife."

After Miss Lucy went to bed that night, they slipped away and stayed aboard the houseboat in each others' arms. They made plans for the future until almost dawn, when they were finally lulled to sleep listening to small waves lap against the bulkhead.

Early that morning Miss Lucy walked into the kitchen and found Bill and Delia making breakfast.

"Well, what're you two doing up so early and smiling like panther cats?"

"You are looking at the happiest man on the island," said Bill. "Delia has consented to marry me."

"Well, it's about time. I've been 'specting it. I knew you two loved each other better'n Peter loved the Lord. We'll have a broom jumping 'cause we never know when a preacher will show. I'm gonna perform the ceremony instead of Percy. And I'll take my tea when I come back from the privy," she said as she and Sooner headed for the back door.

"What in the hell is a broom jumping?" Bill asked after the door slammed to.

"Let Miss Lucy tell you," Delia said, laughing. "It's hard to believe."

Miss Lucy returned and asked for her yaupon. When Bill poured her a cup, she took a sip and let out a yell, "Gaud a'mighty! It's hotter than the hinges of hell. You must've boiled it over pine pitch."

Bill apologized and said, "Delia told me what happened to her in Beaufort and it's best she doesn't go with me until I straighten out her problem. When I return we plan to leave for Charleston and be married there."

"Why don't you get hitched here before you leave? I know what's going to happen by the way you two eyeball each other, and we ain't having no sand wrestling or weed thrashing until you get hitched. You two look like you could swallow each other—and give you ten years and you'll wish to Gaud you had."

After she explained the ceremony to Bill, they decided to appease her by agreeing to a broomstick wedding. Plans were made for the next Saturday.

The wedding took place in Miss Lucy's front yard under a large oak tree dripping with Spanish moss. All the islanders were invited and all attended, except Percy. Delia and Bill, holding hands, started to jump. "Damn!" yelled Bill. "What was that?" A curlew bird flew by their heads and landed on a low tree branch nearby. It started screaming its flight call: *kli-li-li-li.*

"Oh Gaud!" said Miss Lucy. "Somebody shoo that bird out of that tree. It's a bad omen if a curlew lights and utters its flight song, and a good omen if it sings while in flight. I've never seen a curlew fly that close before."

Delia took special note of the bird and Miss Lucy's remark about a bad omen, and it bothered her. Was it one of the superstitions she was used to hearing around the island, or was it something greater? She tended to believe it was some kind of outside force intervening in her life, independent of anything she could do. It was her instinct to approach the curlew and reach out to it. What was it trying to say? She shifted her attention back to the ceremony and they accomplished the jump without a hitch.

After Miss Lucy pronounced them man and wife according to island law, she said, "Ya'll form a line and march into the house fer yaupon tea, wild grape wine, and sugar cookies. Go easy on the wine. I made it meself and too much will cross both yer eyes. Wipe yer feet afore going into the house. And ya'll in fishing boots, leave them at the door."

Bill and Delia spent their honeymoon walking on the beach and swimming in the surf. Nights were spent aboard the houseboat. As Bill expected, it was more than a week before the man came to pilot the boat to Beaufort.

Delia and Miss Lucy walked out on the dock to see him off. He kissed Miss Lucy good-bye, then took Delia in his arms, holding her close until Miss Lucy said, "Gaud a'mighty Bill, turn her loose afore ye break a rib or two. You Yankees sho' love to slobber."

They watched and waved good-bye until the boat cleared the mouth of Silver Lake.

"Let's go, chile. It's bad luck to watch someone go out of sight when they leave." Delia wiped her eyes and followed Miss Lucy home.

CHAPTER EIGHT

The houseboat passed Portsmouth Island and the trip was well underway. Suddenly, the boat ran high on a sand shoal.

"Damn you," Bill said. "You told me you knew every sand shoal between here and Wilmington!"

"Yup, I sho' do, and that is the first one," said Fillmore.

Bill had to go overboard and push while Fillmore ran the motor full power astern. Finally, the keel became clear and they were back in the channel.

"We are returning to Conch Island and you are fired!"

The return was made safely. Two weeks went by before another pilot, named Tooter, was found, but it seemed like two days to Delia and Bill, as they spent the entire time completely absorbed with each other.

Tooter Fulcher had been a pilot most of his life, had never married, and lived a lonely existence on Portsmouth Island. He had retired from the lifesaving station at the cape. He was delighted at the chance to pilot again. Like most islanders, he had his share of pride and enjoyed showing off his expertise with a boat. He acquired the nickname "Tooter" because he frequently blew the whistle on the lifesaving boat when he took it out in the sound. He said he had taken boats to Beaufort many times.

Once more, with tears and good-byes, Bill left for Beaufort, this time with Tooter as his pilot.

Three weeks later the mail boat delivered an official-looking letter addressed to Mr. William Sutton, from an attorney in Mount Kisco, New York. Thinking it might be important, Miss Lucy urged Delia to open it.

"Go ahead and read it. Ain't ye his wife? Ever since I hitched ye, what's his'n is yern and what's yern is his'n. Read it out loud. I want to hear what it has to say."

Delia began to read:

To Mr. William (Bill) Sutton, from Attorney John Jacobs of Mount Kisco.
Dear Sir:
This is to inform you, your sister Heida passed away two months ago and left me guardian of your son William Jr. (nickname Toby). I am physically and financially unable to care for him and I'm sending him to you as soon as I can book him passage to North Carolina.

Delia didn't finish the letter. She felt lightheaded and placed the letter on a table.

"By the look on yer face, I guess that he didn't tell ye he had a son. Why that yaller dog, he is lower'n whale crap!"

"No, he never mentioned he had a son or was ever married. I will keep him until Bill returns. That is, if you will let him stay with us."

"Sho' he can, chile. But wait until I get my paws on that Yankee! I thought he was too good to be true."

86

As the news sank in, Delia began to realize the impact it was having on her. She began to doubt her very nature. *Did I misjudge him? Was I wrong to trust someone so completely without knowing him longer? Why didn't he tell me? He must have had a good reason.* She tried to collect herself before her dreams and hopes became completely unraveled.

It was a month before Toby arrived. Delia met the mail boat expecting to see a small boy, and instead she saw a tall, good-looking youth of maybe thirteen or fourteen. Stepping ashore, he walked up to Delia, extended his hand, and said, "My name is William Sutton Jr., but I'm called Toby. Are you my stepmother?"

"Yes, Toby, and my name is Delia."

"While crossing the sound, Clarence told me about your marriage to my father the island way, whatever that is. He also told me my father is in Beaufort having his houseboat worked on."

Delia was pleased that Toby was attempting to start on a positive note, that he exhibited good manners, and above all, that he showed openness toward her marriage to his father. She confirmed what Toby had heard from Clarence and quickly brought him up to date on remaining news that might interest him.

Gathering up Toby's luggage, which consisted of many expensive-looking pieces, Clarence led the way to Miss Lucy's cottage. Toby arrived first, ran to the front door and stopped dead in his tracks. Standing at the door was Sooner. Toby dropped the luggage he was carrying and bolted for the yard. "What in the world is that animal?" he said from a short distance away.

Miss Lucy appeared in the doorway, "Gaud a'mighty boy, don't ye have raccoons in New York? That animal won't hurt ye. Bring yer bags in."

"That's the largest raccoon I've ever seen, and I've never seen one in a house before."

"Well, ye have now. His name is Sooner. He is three and a great pet. Also, he lets me know when someone comes snooping around. How old are ye, boy? Ye needs some flesh on yer bones 'cause yer downright wormy looking."

"I'm thirteen years old. Everyone says I'm tall for my age, and I am not wormy," he said defensively.

Taking up some of his luggage, he followed Delia into the bedroom that had been previously occupied by his father. With a certain amount of apprehension, Toby noticed that Sooner followed close behind, sniffing at his heels.

During supper, Toby told Delia and Miss Lucy that he had never known his father, and had been led to believe he died when he was born. His mother, originally from France, had died several months ago from cancer. Just before dying, she told him that she had been a maid for several years in his grandfather's home in Mount Kisco, New York, and had fallen madly in love with his father. They had an affair and often met in the loft over the stables. She became pregnant and kept the secret until just before her condition became obvious.

"Oh, Miss Lucy," Delia said, "Bill doesn't know he has a son."

Toby continued, "The gardener helped her leave in the middle of the night for New York City."

Toby went on to say that he was born in a Catholic convent where his mother worked for small wages plus their room and board. There he attended school and sold newspapers in the evenings. Just before his mother died she told him that his father, William Sutton, was alive. She also said she had recently mailed a letter to his father telling that him he had a son and how to find him. Two days later, she died. In the meantime the same gardener, now a caretaker living alone on the estate, received the letter and gave it to Bill's attorney.

When Toby finished, Delia and Miss Lucy were teary-eyed. "Well, son, ye have a home now," Miss Lucy said, wiping her eyes. Delia thanked him for sharing his sad life with them.

A month passed and Toby adjusted to his new life. Like his father, his friendly demeanor made it easy to make friends. It didn't take long to find a few boys his age. On one occasion some of his friends took him on his first flounder gigging trip. They laughed at his ignorance while they tried to teach him how to gig the fish. He took their remarks good-naturedly and always had an answer for them.

Tim, who was the largest boy and a bully, said, "Yankee, the fust thing is ye don't go in the sound dressed finer'n a New Bern lawyer. And when I tell ye thar lies a flounder, ye stab it right betwixt the eyes, not the middle of its back or its tail. And you don't try to drive a well. I've tol' ye time and agin to quit momicking the fish."

"And I have told you time and again, Johnnie Reb, the only flounder I've ever seen was in a seafood market or on my plate. And by the way, you missed the last two you tried to spear."

"Did you heard that, boys?" said Tim. "He acts mighty biggety. I reckon we oughtta learn him a smidgen of respect fer us islanders."

Picking up the boat pole, he knocked Toby overboard, cutting a gash in Toby's forehead on the skiff's gunwale.

"Now look what ye've done, Tim," Josh Yeomans, a smaller boy, said. "Ye may get outta scrapes, but you'll not get outta this one. Ye had no cause to knock him overboard. I like Toby. He's my friend and a nice Yankee . . . "

Later that day, the two friends arrived at Miss Lucy's. Toby, afraid of being reprimanded for fighting, slipped in the back door and made for his room to change his wet clothes and wash the blood from his face. Josh related what happened to Delia and Miss Lucy.

"It sho' was somethin' to see, Miss Delia. With blood running down his face and hellfire in his eyes, Toby climbed back aboard, knocked Tim to the bottom of the skiff and nigh on beat the p'licker out of him. The last we saw of Tim he was running fer home with two purty black eyes, a cut lip, and smeared with flounder slime. You could hear him holler a mile away. He won't mess with Toby anymore."

"That had to be Tim Wayhab that Toby tangled with," said Miss Lucy. "He has always been meaner'n a rattlesnake, and chews 'backer jest like a mountaineer. Come out here, boy, let's see what ye look like."

Toby came to the door holding a rag to his bloody forehead.

"Gaud a'mighty son, ye gotta a bad cut," Miss Lucy said. "Josh, run to the woodshed and bring a handful of clean spider webs. I saw some in the woodshed the other day. And Delia, cut some rags from that old white bedsheet."

Several minutes later Josh ran in and handed Miss Lucy the spider webs. "Most all I seed were clean. The spiders left 'cause they hadn't caught a single fly or bug. I bets dem spiders are some kinda' hungry."

Miss Lucy saw the frown on Toby's face when she started to apply the webs to his wound and said, "This won't hurt, it's an old-time method we folks use to stop the bleeding. Ye po' boy, I hope ye momicked that Tim good-fashioned.

"After I finish dressing yer cut, how about ye two go and fetch that flounder ya'll gigged. We'll bake it fer supper. And don't get any fish slime in that cut, or it won't heal afore yer father comes back . . . if he ever does," she added as Josh and Toby went out the door.

"By the way Delia, wonder what's happened to yer Bill? He's been gone over two months. Gaud a'mighty, he's had enough time to build three boats."

"I've been thinking the same thing," said Delia. "Why hasn't he returned or sent a letter or something telling why he's being detained?"

An hour after Bill and Tooter left, they stopped at the only store on Sea Island for kerosene for the generator. The small weather-beaten store leaned precariously backward—the result of several storms. The few sparsely stocked shelves displayed mostly fishing gear.

They purchased the kerosene, which they pumped from a barrel outside. Bill left Tooter gabbing with a few old men sitting outside on a bench that leaned up against the front of the store. Some were whittling, others chewed tobacco and spit or spun yarns. Bill wasn't out of hearing range when he heard one of the men say, "Tooter, ye must be hard up to hire on with an ickypoo Yankee. That boat is something else. Never seed the likes of her."

"Cap'n Bill ain't one of them thar highfalutin' Yankees," Tooter said. "The folks on Conch Island like him, and so do I. Besides, he pays good."

Bill showed his lack of interest in their conversation by heading back toward his boat. Moreover, he was slightly nervous about being tied up to a crudely constructed dock. On his way back he met a man carrying a Canadian goose decoy. The feathers were painted on gray canvas, with the neck and head beautifully carved out of wood and painted in a very life-like manner.

"What a beauty," Bill said to the man. "Out in the water I wouldn't be able to tell the decoy from a real goose. Where did you find such a beautiful work of art?"

"I made her meself," the man said. "I make lots and sell them to Yankees that come down fer fall hunting. Would ye like this one? I have more at home."

"How much would you charge for that one?" Bill asked.

"I gets twenty dollars and sometimes more. Fer you, I'll take twenty."

"How about fifteen?"

"Well, so I won't have to carry this one back home, I'll take it."

"That's my houseboat tied to that dock, and my name is Bill Sutton," he said and handed the man a twenty-dollar bill. "Do you have change for this?

"No sir, but ye can take the goose to yer boat and I'll take yer money to the store and bring back yer five dollars."

An hour later Tooter returned and handed Bill an unusual-looking paper.

"Here are the five confederate dollars Henry said ye wanted. He tol' ye to keep them, and that the South shall rise agin. I don't know what ye want them fer. They've not been worth a tinkers damn now that the war is over."

"He was supposed to change my twenty dollars at the store and bring me back five dollars," Bill said, laughing. "But I shall keep this for a souvenir."

"How much did he want fer that goose?" Tooter asked.

"He wanted twenty, but I told him fifteen."

"Oh yeah, he sho' skinned ye," said Tooter. "He has never gotten over five or six fer a goose. I would go get yer money, but the tide is ebbing fast and if we don't untie and get out of here in the next thirty minutes, the boat will be listing forty-five degrees starboard and her keel will be showing."

As they pulled away from Sea Island, Tooter ran the motor almost idle as the ebb tide carried them swiftly along until the sound narrowed in width. The small channel, with its many S curves around the marsh grass, made navigation tedious.

They were rounding a curve close to the bank's shore when Tooter said, "Cap'n, I think we best run her bow ashore and anchor the stern off until the tide changes. She draws too much water fer that curve up ahead. The tide is almost slack, and when it starts to flood agin we can get underway. I'd say in about an hour."

"That's fine with me, Tooter. I would like to step ashore and look around."

"I don't know, Cap'n, they is some wild horses on that island. Thar's one stallion that's blacker'n the hinges of hell and meaner'n a cut billy goat. A man from Harkers Island tried to rope him and got the living daylights kicked outta him. Then the horse chased him into the channel."

Bill thought about Delia telling him about the horses and how they arrived on Shackleford Banks. *Could this be the horse that saved Delia's life?*

Tooter ran the bow ashore and secured the stern line to keep the boat from swinging around against the marsh. He decided he would lay down for a short nap. Grabbing crackers and a soda, Bill jumped ashore, scattering fiddler crabs in all directions. Reaching the top of a sand dune, he could see both sides of Shackleford Banks, from Taylor's Cut to the ocean. A small group of horses, led by a beautiful black stallion, emerged from a group of trees and headed toward a pond.

Bill crept slowly toward them. Suddenly one of the mares looked up, gave a loud neigh and, followed by the other mares, ran in the opposite direction. The black stallion, which could have been Delia's Duke, made right for him, kicking and neighing as he came. Bill ran back toward the sand dune but the stallion outran him, knocked him down, turned, and joined his mares.

An hour later, Tooter awoke from his nap. The tide was high enough for them to leave, but Bill was nowhere to be seen. Tooter jumped from the boat and ran toward the dune where he last saw Bill. When he reached the top of the dune, there was Bill, stretched out. Tooter thought he was taking a nap.

"Hey Cap'n!" he yelled. "Damn these Yankees! You never know what crazy things they might do. Hey Cap'n!" he yelled again. "Let's go, we need to get underway." There was no answer. He ran down to where Bill was lying, unconscious but still breathing. All around him were fresh hoof tracks. After several attempts to rouse him, he threw Bill across his shoulders and headed back to the boat.

"Thank Gaud fer high tide," he said, and ran the throttle full choke the rest of the way to Beaufort. When the boat bumped the dock, Bill opened his eyes.

"Well, we made it fast.. Don't you move, Cap'n Bill. I'm going to find Dr. Mason."

Five minutes later Tooter burst into Dr. Mason's office. "I need a doctor," he said breathlessly. "I have a man a horse has kicked the p'licker out of."

The doctor followed Tooter to the houseboat and said Bill had a concussion and a couple of broken ribs. After doing what the doctor could do for him there, they carried him, with the help of two other men, to Mrs. Willis' waterfront boardinghouse.

It was the next morning before Bill opened his eyes and saw Tooter sitting in a chair by the window. "What happened and who are you?" he asked.

"It's me, Cap'n. Ye know—Tooter. Oh Gaud, the man is loony." He bolted for the door and ran for Dr. Mason. He wasn't as lucky in finding him this time. He searched the local taverns until he finally found the doctor in one, drinking ale and playing poker with several rowdy-looking seamen.

"Doc! Come quick, the cap'n is awake and I don't believe he knows me from Adam's house cat."

Back at the boardinghouse, they discovered Bill couldn't remember his name or anything about his previous life.

"He has amnesia," said Dr. Mason, "from the lick on his head. Maybe he will regain his memory in a few days, but then it may take years—or never." Turning to Tooter, he asked, "Do you know anything about his family? What island did you two leave from?"

"His name is Bill Sutton. I signed on as his pilot at Conch Island. He don't talk about hisself. That's I all know."

Finding no identification on Bill, Dr. Mason suggested they go aboard the houseboat to see if there was an address of someone they could contact.

Rummaging through Bill's desk, they found over two hundred dollars and some letters that were ruined during the hurricane and unreadable.

"Well, I think this man must be financially well-to-do to have such a nice boat," said Dr. Mason.

"I'm getting outta here on the first boat that leaves the dock," said Tooter, "afore someone starts a tale that I knocked him in his head fer his money. I'll not set foot on Conch Island again." Grabbing his cap, he rushed out the door.

CHAPTER NINE

Two months after Bill left the island, Delia realized that she was pregnant. Suspecting something had happened to Bill and that he wasn't coming back to the island, several frantic thoughts passed through her mind. *How can I provide for a child? Oh God, what will I do? Did he intend to leave me?* Then, she wondered if she wasn't thinking only of herself—maybe he was injured or even dead. Suddenly, she felt completely helpless and at that moment, it seemed that her world was breaking apart. After surviving several unbelievable crises, she had retained some degree of hope that Bill would return and that their lives would continue on together somewhere—maybe England.

Destiny, she thought. *It was all meant to be and there isn't much I can do about it. Isn't that what Father would say?*

She recalled that before Bill arrived on the island, Percy had approached her on several occasions, asking if she could help run the store and post office. He wanted her near so he could keep his eye on her. With clerking at the store on her mind, and prior to mentioning her pregnancy to Miss Lucy, she looked for Percy in order to apply for the job. She found him in the back of the small, dirty store, asleep in a chair.

"Percy, I will work in the store for you for fifteen dollars a week. I'll work half a day on Saturday, but I need Sunday off. And if you try any monkey business, I will quit. Is that clear?"

"Well now, guess you have come off yer high horse since that highfalutin' Yankee left ye high and dry," Percy said with a smirk. "I'll give ye ten dollars a week."

"That is not enough." Turning around, she started to walk out.

"All right, I'll make it fifteen. And you start tomorrow."

Delia waited until after supper to tell Miss Lucy about her pregnancy and the job at the store.

Miss Lucy reacted to the news with an uncharacteristic hug.

"Oh chile, don't you worry. We will manage. I think it would be nice to have a baby around the house. Why not wait fer Bill a little while longer before you go to work fer that horny bastard Percy? I think maybe Bill is sick and you will hear from him soon."

"Maybe so, but do you believe he's dead?" Delia asked. Miss Lucy didn't answer and sopped up her molasses with cornbread.

It was early autumn and preparations were being made for the new school teacher's arrival. Delia closed the store to help clean the schoolhouse and the teacher's living quarters. The school term for the year ran from September until January, with no more than thirty children attending from the first to the seventh grade.

The one room clapboard schoolhouse on the edge of the village had its own two-room teacher's living quarters attached. The structure was built from shipwreck salvage, including a ship's bell hanging from a post by the door. In the back of the schoolhouse, spaced several yards apart, were two one-hole privies. Someone had painted "buoys" on one door and "gulls" on the other. Myrtle bushes surrounded the girl's privy so the boys couldn't peek.

Amusing conversations bantered about, helping Delia keep her mind off her situation.

"I wonder what this year's teacher will be like," said one woman while dusting the bureau in the bedroom quarters. "I sho' didn't care fer that last one. She momicked my Jess all year jest 'cause he put two lizards in her bedcovers."

"Yeah, how about the time he put a dead crab in her desk drawer?" another woman asked.

"My Jess said he didn't do that, but he got the blame. Why don't ye tell of the time yer youngern put turpentine all over her desk cheer seat and she was begombed fer a week?"

Another said, "How's about the time she found head lice on my Tom's head and doused all the youngerns heads with hog's lard and sulfur, then everyday made the youngerns comb their heads with a fine-tooth comb?"

"Why don't ye shet up yer jawing and get to work, or we'll be here all day." said the oldest woman.

While the women were cleaning and dusting, the men were out back cutting firewood for the two stoves—the kitchen stove and the potbelly one in the middle of the school-room. Two of the men discussed the new teacher as they split logs: "I sho' hope this new teacher is purty. That last one was ugly! Ugly! She had a nose on her large as a bilge pump."

"Yeah, and she sho' stunk from that asafetida bag she wore around her neck to ward off them germs she thought we had, and she was the one that looked wormy. 'Sides that, she had buck teeth."

Several days later Delia was working in the store when a tall, scrawny stranger staggered through the doorway carrying so much stuff she could barely see his face. His eyeglasses were lopsided and hanging almost to the end of his nose. Delia couldn't help laughing.

"Lady, I don't see anything funny about this. I was told when I left New Bern someone would meet me at the dock and help with my gear. Where is everyone, for God's sake? My name is Mike Simpson. I'm from Eden. I was hired by the state to be this year's teacher. If I had known this place was so isolated and barren, I wouldn't have consented to come."

"Mr. Simpson, my name is Delia Sutton, and the reason no one met you is that everyone is on the ocean side of the island, salting mullets. The men caught a big school this morning. It's the first fall run. If you've never been to the islands before—and you can stick around long enough, which I doubt—they will teach you something instead of you teaching them." *The nerve of this guy,* she thought.

Her conversation was interrupted when a young boy came running into the store. Taking a while to catch his breath, he managed to say, "Miss Delia! Come quick. A stingray stung Toby and the barb is still in his leg. He was helping Papa pull a fishnet ashore, and must've stepped on it. Papa is bringing him home now—"

Leaving the boy and teacher, Delia dashed out the door and met Zeke and several men carrying Toby. His trousers were split above his knee and she could see two inches of the stingray's barb protruding from the calf of his leg. He was in lots of pain and his face was two shades lighter than usual.

The men carried Toby in the house and turned him over to Miss Lucy. She examined the wound and called Delia aside. "Chile, that sting is full of poison and has to be cut out now. It's going to hurt like hell. Thar is no pulling it out because the barbs on the sting are like an arrowhead—jest opposite from the way it entered. Zeke and I have taken them out before, but they weren't deep as this one."

100

"Couldn't we take him to the doctor on the mainland?" Delia asked, crying.

"No. He would have gangrene before we could get him thar and most likely his leg would have to be removed."

Miss Lucy took over and began to give orders. "Everyone get out except Zeke and two of ye strong men. Delia, ye go in the kitchen, build a fire, and put on a kettle of water. Zeke, get the laudanum out of my medicine box and give Toby a dose. Then take that big knife from the kitchen shelf and go outside to the whetstone. When ye can cut a hair with it, bring the blasted thing in and heat it in the kitchen stove 'til it glows. I'll round up some clean rags. Now get to work, dammit. Don't keep standing around like dead wood!"

When Toby became groggy from the effects of the laudanum and all the necessary items were placed by the bedside, Miss Lucy made Delia leave the room. She then put a rag in Toby's mouth. Kissing him on the cheek, she whispered, "Now son, when I say go, I want ye to bite down on this rag, hard. I'll remove this damn barb as gently and quick as I can." Turning to the two men, she said, "Each of ye hold a leg steady with all yer might and don't let go until I tell ye." Picking up the knife and dipping it in kerosene, she said, "Go" and started the incision. When the knife entered his flesh, Toby screamed and bit down on the rag as the two men held his legs. When Miss Lucy removed the barb, it left a round hole in his leg the size of her thumb. She then poured turpentine in the wound to wash out the sting slime.

"That will keep it from being sore and also stop the infection," Miss Lucy said to Delia, who had entered the room. "The hole has to heal from the bottom up. Zeke, go see if you can find some sulfur."

Miss Lucy's remedies and efforts were not enough. Days went by and the wound became infected to the extent that it smelled like rotten flesh. Miss Lucy covered it with a slab of salt pork called fat back, and covered it with a collard leaf to draw out the poison. Delia was told the salt did the drawing and the collard leaf kept it moist.

"We use this method to draw poison from wounds or bring boils to a head," Miss Lucy said.

Several days later Toby began to run a fever. When red streaks appeared on his leg, Miss Lucy called Delia into the kitchen. "Chile, I've done all I know to do. He needs a doctor, and fast. Go get someone from the lifesaving station to take him to New Bern. I jest hope it ain't too late. Now stop that whimpering and gits. You won't be worth a tinkers damn, so I'll go with him."

By the time Miss Lucy packed a few clothes for herself and Toby, Delia returned with two men from the lifesaving station. They had hardly cleared the door before Miss Lucy was giving out orders, as usual. "I want ye to put Toby in this straight back cheer and carry him to the boat. He mustn't walk on that leg, and if ye drop him I'll skin ye and tack yer hide to the side of my privy."

Turning to Delia, she said, "Chile, you best stay here in case yer Bill comes or ye hear from him. I'll return as soon as my Sawbones fixes Toby up. Ye can come to the pier with us, but fer Toby's sake, I don't want any whimpering when we leave. And don't ye worry none, if the sound is rough when we cross over, his leg won't hurt. I dowsed him good with laudanum while ye were in the kitchen."

Toby slept all the way to New Bern. Arriving late that afternoon, they found Dr. Maxwell with his last patient for the day. When the same nurse that previously attended Miss Lucy came to the door and saw Miss Lucy and Toby, she left in a hurry to tell the doctor they were there. "Doctor, you better come quick. That same woman that called you 'Sawbones' is here. You know she won't wait long."

The door swung open. "Well, if it isn't Miss Lucy," said Dr. Maxwell, "the icon of Conch Island. Did you come to bring me a mess of mullet pluck?"

"No, but I'll pluck ye if ye don't see to this boy right now! He was stung by a damn stingray."

"I see removing your flues, as you called it, hasn't improved your disposition. Let's take the lad into my examining room. Miss Lucy, you stay put. I don't want you cussing me if he grunts the first time."

Thirty minutes later Dr. Maxwell came out and, taking Miss Lucy by the hand, led her to a chair and explained the situation. "I have some bad news, but it's not all bad."

"Gaud a'mighty, Sawbones, I've been on pins and needles while you were in thar. So fer Gaud's sake, out with your spiel."

"The bad news is the tip of the stingray barb broke off and is embedded at the bottom of the wound. He has a bad case of gangrene as far up as the knee. If the leg isn't removed up to his kneecap, he will die within forty-eight hours. If we remove it immediately, he will live."

"Did you tell Toby?"

"Yes I did, and that is one brave lad. He said whatever you decided would be all right with him."

Early the next morning, after working all night to reduce Toby's fever, Dr. Maxwell removed Toby's leg at the knee joint. Coming out of the operating room, he found Miss Lucy sitting by the door with tears running down her cheeks. Taking her in his arms, he said, "My dear, I didn't think I would ever see you cry. You were always so strong and independent. What relation is the lad to you?"

"None," she replied. "He is Delia's stepson and I've more or less adopted both of them. And I want you to know I'm still strong, independent and meaner'n a bore hog. When can I take Toby back to the island?"

"In a few days, if there are no complications. He is a very weak lad."

Lucy asked the nurse to bring her a cot for Toby's room, and said that she was going to sleep there. The nurse told her that wasn't allowed.

"Well, we'll see about that, Miss Fancy Pants—if you could find a pair to fit you." The nurse left in a huff to look for Dr. Maxwell.

When Dr. Maxwell told her she could sleep in Toby's room, she said, "Sawbones, why don't you get shed of that woman. She is ugly. My raccoon's stern would make her a Sunday face."

Two days later Toby developed a cold and a high fever. The fifth day he died of pneumonia as Miss Lucy held him in her arms. She was devastated to the extent that Dr. Maxwell had to take care of all the arrangements. He first sent a wireless message to Delia, via the island lifesaving station, telling her the circumstances involving Toby's death, and that Miss Lucy and the body would return to the island the following day.

Dr. Maxwell had his arm around Miss Lucy as they followed the casket to the pier. She declined his invitation to accompany her home, saying she would be all right and would rather face Delia alone. As he helped her aboard the boat, she kissed him good-bye and said, "Thank you, Doctor, fer being so good to me. I couldn't have managed without ye. If'n yer wife dies afore ye, how about giving me a chance? I'm not getting any older, I'm jest getting better. 'Sides, antiques are valuable."

"Why Miss Lucy, you flatter me. And that's the first time you haven't called me Old Sawbones. I think you're turning into a dignified Southern lady."

"Gaud a'mighty, Sawbones, don't you know that would ruin my rep'tation on the isand? I have to stay tougher'n whale lips to keep the folks on the island in line. That's why they call me Queenie behind my back."

A couple of men tied the casket to the top of the boat's pilothouse, then draped a black sail across the bow and down to the water line to let other boats know it was a funeral barge. When funeral boats approached, motors stopped and vessels drifted until the barge passed by. It was considered bad luck not to do so.

As the boat was pulling away from the pier, Miss Lucy yelled to Dr. Maxwell, "Don't forget, Sawbones, you promised to come and spend yer vacation with us. I'll feed ye some straight up and down food and put a little fat on yer bones."

"I promise," he answered, and stood waving until the boat was almost out of sight.

The return trip from New Bern took twice as long as usual. It was considered disrespectful to run a funeral barge full throttle. Hours later, the island appeared far ahead of them as a silhouette in the moonlight. When the boat entered the lake Miss Lucy heard Zeke blowing the conch shell, announcing the arrival of Toby's body. The news of his death had spread across the island like wildfire—the islanders knew at almost the same time Delia received Dr. Maxwell's wire.

As the boat slowly approached the pier, a group of men and women paid homage by singing, "We shall gather at the river." Delia stood off to the side, crying. Stepping on the pier, Miss Lucy took Delia in her arms and they both stood crying while the men lifted the casket to their shoulders and carried it down the pier. They walked to Miss Lucy's house and placed it in the middle of her parlor, where the wake would be held. Two candles were lit and placed at the head of the casket. The lid was opened and would be left that way until just before the burial. This was for the viewing of the corpse, and for Toby's spirit to know he was home and loved.

Just before midnight, Miss Lucy ran everyone home except Zeke and Walter, who were ordered to sit with the body the rest of the night. When they were about to refuse, she said, "I insist ye stay and I want one of ye in here at all times. I'll be checking on ye during the night. When the candles burn down, thar are more on the table. I'm plum wore out, the worst I've ever been. I'm going to rest now."

Two hours later, Zeke, thinking Walter was asleep in the chair, tiptoed toward the door. "Whar do ye think yer going?" whispered Walter. "Yer not leaving me alone with a dead body!"

"I'm going to the privy. We both can't leave, or Miss Lucy will lambaste us fer sure."

"I've got to go too," said Walter. "We both can go off the corner of the porch." While the men relieved themselves, Sooner jumped in the casket, curled up at the foot and went to sleep.

Sometime later, both men were nodding in their ladder-back chairs, leaning against the wall, when Walter all of a sudden came crashing down in his chair. "Zeeeeke, did you hear that thumping sound in the coffin?!"

"No, you are getting . . ." BANG, the coffin lid came down and Sooner started chattering. Both men jumped and simultaneously dashed for the door, wedging themselves in the doorway. They kicked, swore, and tore at each other's clothes until they knocked the door loose from its hinges and were free, but not without a price. Walter was forced to run through the village without his trousers, which were ripped off on the door hinge. His appearance was not on his mind, though, as he climbed the few steps to his porch and fell down sprawling, out of breath. He felt two strong arms pick him up, and looked up in his wife's face before focusing on his nearly naked body; trouble was trouble.

Sure enough, she accused him of fooling around with another woman and he had to leave in a hurry. It wasn't until his wife heard the whole story from Zeke that he was allowed back in the house.

Before Zeke reached his front yard he was heard yelling, "Bring me a clean pair trousers, woman, 'cause these are begombed. We've had the p'licker skeered out of us by Toby's hant."

The next day, Miss Lucy conducted a short funeral in her front yard. They buried Toby under the live oak tree next to Miss Lucy's husband. Following the eulogy and the recitation of the Lord's Prayer, a simple grave marker carved out of cedar was placed at the head of his grave with a single inscription: *Toby Sutton.*

Toby's death coincided with Delia's seventh month of pregnancy. The fact that she hadn't gained much weight, making it difficult to detect whether or not she was pregnant, carried with it a mixed blessing. On one hand, she was happy she was able to continue working for Percy because she needed money to pay for Toby's doctor and funeral bills; on the other hand, she continually had to ward off Percy's sexual advances. Her overpowering need for money dictated her decision not to tell Miss Lucy about Percy's behavior. But this was Conch Island, where rumors traveled and spread like brushfires on a hot summer day.

One day Miss Lucy and a neighbor, Mary, were out gathering yaupon leaves. Without showing the slightest amount of self-restraint, Mary made the comment, "You know, that

Percy is one horny bastard. They say he tried to mess with
Delia yestiddy and she ran him out of the store with a broom."
In her blunt, sardonic way, she added that Percy tol' her husband Walter that he tapped Delia last summer on the beach
and that she is going to have his youngern come spring.

Dropping her apron full of yaupon leaves, Miss Lucy ran
for the store, hoping to find Percy there.

"Dammit, where is that scum bum of a Percy?" she gasped
as she stumbled through the doorway.

"Miss Lucy, you shouldn't run like that. You are out of
breath. What has happened?" Delia asked.

"I'll tell ye what that lying Percy said about ye on the way
home. Like the Good Book says, 'The jawbone of an ass is
dangerous.' Shet down this shack of a store, 'cause ye are
through working fer that bastard."

"But I need the money for Toby's bills. And don't you
worry, because I can handle Percy."

"Come, chile, we are going home and see if thar ain't some
money in those last letters that came fer Bill. Thar ain't been
any mail fer him in over three months. He is not coming back
or he is dead. Ye are his wife, so now they're yern."

The first letter Delia opened was from the Chesapeake
Railroad and contained a dividend check for five hundred
dollars. Several more letters were from friends and the last one,
from a New York firm, contained a check for six hundred
dollars.

"Gaud a'mighty, that's the most money I've seen at one
time in my whole life," said Miss Lucy.

"But what do I do with it?" said Delia. "How am I going
to get it cashed? I've never cashed or written a check in my
life."

"Chile, let me tell you what to do. First, sign Bill's name
on the back of the check and then your name, Mrs. Delia
Sutton, underneath. Then we will mail it to Dr. Maxwell in

New Bern, along with a letter asking him to deposit it in the bank under your name. My government pension check is sent to that same bank. Then, when he returns your checkbook, you can pay off all Toby's bills and have enough left so you don't have to work fer that damn Percy. Now, get a pencil and some paper and write what I have to say."

It was a week before the mail boat arrived. Miss Lucy met the boat and gave the letter to Clarence with instructions to hand-carry it to Dr. Maxwell. He was then to bring back a note from the doctor saying that the letter had been received. Miss Lucy gave him two dollars for a case of Sweet Society snuff, and promised to pay him twenty cents for his trouble when he returned. Delia hoped that the letter would arrive; since letters she mailed to London were never answered, she had little faith in the postal system.

A week later Miss Lucy was stooped over, worming her collards and singing "The Old Rugged Cross," when she was grabbed around her waist from behind. She exploded up from the ground with such velocity that she pulled up a whole collard plant and fell over backwards, knocking her assailant flat on the ground. She fell on top of him and began beating him with the collard stalk.

"Miss Lucy! Miss Lucy!" Delia screamed. "It's Dr. Maxwell."

"Gaud a' mighty, Sawbones, ye have skeered the p'licker out of me! Where in the world did ye come from?"

"Well, we are even, fer you have beat the p'licker out of me. I shouldn't have slipped up on you like that. I came on the mail boat to pay you that visit I promised. Do you remember?"

"Hell yes, I remember. Ye might have taken my flues but I still have my head, and my health is holding up tolerable well.

109

Sho' glad to see ye, Sawbones." Turning to Delia, she said, "Chile, grab a mess of these collard leaves and we will have them fer dinner if thar is enough salt pork left to boil them in. It takes a slap of pork big as a horse's arse and lots of water to make good collards."

After Dr. Maxwell showed Delia how to write the checks for Toby's bills, he asked her when she was expecting the baby. "There isn't a doctor on the island, so if you will come to New Bern I will be glad to deliver the baby for you."

Overhearing, Miss Lucy said, "Thanks Sawbones, but we have Maud Wayhab. She has birthed all the babies on the island fer the last thirty years and helped her mother before that. She has a damn good record, losing two in all these years, and they were stillborn. I remember one year . . . "

Delia and Dr. Maxwell looked at each other, smiled, and settled back in their chairs, waiting for her to reminisce, knowing she was determined to live up to her reputation as a "tootsie teller"—the islander's word for storyteller.

She took a dip of snuff, crossed her ankles and continued, "Several small youngerns kept pestering Maud about where babies came from 'cause they wanted a baby too. Finally, one day she told them she dug babies out of a turnip patch. Before those youngerns were caught, they dug up half the turnips on the island. Thar weren't many folks eating turnips that spring."

"She should've told them the truth," said Delia.

"Sawbones, have ye ever heard of a blue caul?" Miss Lucy asked.

"Yes, I have, but in medical terms it's known as amnion. Why do you ask?"

"Well, Maud said her mother tol' her of birthing a baby years ago with jest sech a caul, named Lola Meekins. The story goes she conjured her husband, Wes Meekins, when she caught him messing around with a tart named Eddie—the menfolk called her 'Round Heels'—said a man jest blew his breath in her face and she fell flat on her back."

"Come, Miss Lucy, you don't believe there is such a thing as conjuring," said Delia.

"Wait, I ain't finished," said Lucy. "The night Lola caught them, a strange dog and cat were seen walking the beach, howling at the moon. The next day someone in the village saw a dead dog and cat at the inlet. Of course the animals could have fallen from a boat or been thrown overboard and washed ashore, especially since it was blowing a nose skinner to the east the night Wes and Eddie disappeared, along with Wes' skiff. Others said they were trying to escape when the boat capsized and they drowned. Or they made it to the mainland and disappeared. They, nor the skiff, ain't been seen since. Lola died a year later from a black widow spider bite. I ain't saying fer sure the tale I heard is true, and I ain't saying it ain't."

Dr. Maxwell had been on the island exactly one week when they heard the mail boat's whistle blowing as she pulled up to the village dock. A young boy brought a message from Clarence saying that if the doctor wanted to go to the mainland, the boat would be leaving shortly.

"This has been a delightful vacation," Dr. Maxwell said. "Thanks, Miss Lucy, for inviting me. If I had known the island was such a beautiful and pleasant place I would have visited much sooner. I plan to retire in the near future and would love to come here and open a small clinic and hotel, if the islanders wouldn't mind. What do you think, Miss Lucy?"

"Bless yer heart, Sawbones, that's the best idea ye've ever had. The folks herebouts would be happier'n a rooster in a barnyard full of hens. Jest don't take away folks asafetida or turpentine on a spoon of sugar fer a cough."

"That's settled then. Is there anything I can send you from New Bern?"

"I need two quarts of store-bought licker, called Southern Comfort, to mix with my asafetida. That last quart of moonshine they brought me from the mainland would eat the bottom out of a chamber pot. Come wintertime I drink a swig every morning 'cause it helps my rheumatis."

"You need to replenish your asafetida also," said Delia. "That in the bottom of your jar looks like it's at least ten years old, and I never see you shake the jar when you take a swig, regardless of what season it is. What she is doing, Dr. Maxwell, is drinking pure liquor. She had rather die than have the islanders know she loves her liquor. And don't worry, Miss Lucy, I had rather die than tell on you."

"Gaud a'mighty gal, asafetida and my snuff is all the pleasure I gets out of life. So jest stop yer meddling."

Dr. Maxwell laughed, "Don't worry, Delia. At her age it won't hurt her to have a little liquor once or twice a day."

"Thank you, Sawbones, and let's make that a case of Southern Comfort. I'll pay ye when I get it."

On Clarence's next trip from the mainland, he brought a case of Southern Comfort for Miss Lucy and a case of English tea for Delia.

A few days later Miss Lucy and Delia were in the yard hanging out clothes, when they heard thunder rumbling.

"That thundersquall is coming from the southwest," said Miss Lucy. "That's a good sign dog days is upon us. We need rain real bad, fer it sure has been a dry spell. I want it to rain enough to make Noah's flood look like a morning dew. You know I'm jest joshing. When we have a lot of rain it brings out swarms of them damn gallynippers, with a heads big as field peas. The folks on the mainland call them mosquitoes."

"Miss Lucy, how you do exaggerate."

"I know, but we best gather pine straw fer the smoke pot and give those bugs a dose of smoke."

The storm drew near as they hurried to gather the straw. Miss Lucy was stooping over to fill her apron when a strong wind, preceding the rapidly approaching storm, knocked her over. Delia ran to help her up as a bolt of lightning struck a pine tree nearby, splitting it from top to bottom and scattering splinters of wood in all directions. Simultaneously, there was a deafening clap of thunder followed by a strong smell of brimstone and turpentine. With the noise of the thunderbolt still ringing in their ears, they made it inside the house.

Delia was pulling pine splinters out of Miss Lucy's bonnet when she screamed, "Gaud a'mighty, Sooner was in the yard with us." Running to the window, she saw Sooner on the ground, hairless, with all four feet in the air, near the pine tree that had been struck by lightning. Delia tried to stop Miss Lucy as she made a dash for the door and ran in the downpour toward the raccoon. She picked Sooner up, wrapped him in her apron and stumbled back to the house, yelling for Delia to fetch some clean towels.

"This critter is out like a light—but still alive," Miss Lucy said with tears streaming down her cheeks. "Bring me my asafetida bottle. A dose of that should bring him around." Prying open his mouth, she poured half a cup of her asafetida down his throat. A few minutes later he jumped from her lap, made about two laps around the room and, after several somersaults, ran under the table. "Gaud a' mighty, I do believe Sooner is tipsy," Miss Lucy said, laughing. It was hard to tell if he was a raccoon or a skinned monkey. The most severe burn left a streak down his back.

Miss Lucy spent most of the night knitting a pair of pants and a jacket for the critter. Whenever he needed to go outdoors, she would remove his pants and let him out. He stayed outside just long enough to relieve himself. Then he would return, scratching on the door to come back inside. It took two months for his hair to grow two inches. In the meantime, he resembled a fuzz ball. When his hair finally grew back there was a white streak down his back from his head to his tail, giving him the appearance of a skunk.

A month later, in the middle of the night, Delia's water broke. She waited until daybreak before she told Miss Lucy she was going into labor and that it was time to contact Maud. Contractions were then three minutes apart. Having had one baby, Delia knew what to expect and knew to bear down with the pains instead of fighting them. Just before the baby was born, Delia remembered what Rufus told her about the use of snuff, and asked Miss Lucy for her snuffbox so she could put a little under her nose. "Oh Gaud a'mighty!" said Miss Lucy. "The pain has caused the chile to go slam outta her head. They might put it up their nose in England but we put it in our jaw here." A few minutes after Maude administered the snuff, Delia sneezed hard, screamed twice, "Bill! Bill!"—and at 8:05 A.M., a baby boy was born.

"I tell ye Miss Lucy, that gal didn't birth that baby like a Southern lady," said Maud. "She's had a baby before, most likely outta wedlock, 'cause she knew jest what to do and she birthed that youngern too fast."

"You sho' have no room to talk, Maud Wayhab. For I heard you had round heels jest like Eddie, before ye roped yer po' old husband into marriage. And ye didn't cull them either and if that baby ye miscarriaged had lived, it would've looked like Percy. Now gets, ye ain't needed here any longer."

CHAPTER TEN

At 8:05 A.M. that same morning, Bill cried out that a woman had called to him. Taking his second cup of coffee, he went topside and saw no one but Simon, his new pilot. "Where is the lady that just called me?" he asked. Simon stopped polishing a deck rail. "Bossman, thar ain't been a lady around here. Ye must've been dreaming."

"No, I wasn't asleep. I distinctly heard my name called twice. The voice sounded so familiar. Oh well, could be a ghost from my past."

"Don't say that, boss. I's scared to death of ghosts. They say they won't hurt ye, but they will sho' make ye hurt yerself. Cap'n, ye think maybe the voice ye heard was caused by that knock ye got on yer noggin?"

"You could be right," Bill said, returning to the galley.

Bill had hired Simon, a middle-aged black man, after he was recommended by Dr. Mason, who said he had known him for years. Simon, who was in his late fifties, short and bald, and had never married, said all the gals he knew were either too ugly or too fat. He had lived most of his life with his Aunt Bessie and Uncle Joseph after his parents left, during the Civil War, for New York.

Bill enjoyed Simon's Southern cooking and wit. He often took Bill oystering and taught him how to nub clusters of coon oysters into single ones.

A brisk wind faced Bill one day as he took his usual early morning stroll along the dock. When he turned to retrace his steps, he saw a man having difficulty bringing his small sailboat to the town dock. The man might have been a novice sailor, but his problem could have been attributed to the wind and strong ebbing tide. The third time he came around, the man was close enough for Bill to throw him a rope that was tied to a dock cleat. The man pulled himself ashore and, after securing the boat, stepped on the dock. "Thanks fellow," he said, shaking Bill's hand. "I would not have made it without your help. You can tell I'm not an expert sailor or familiar with ebbing tides. My name is George Gorham. I am from up north. I've a couple of friends arriving by yacht this afternoon. We have rented a hunting lodge on Bogue Sound for a month."

Bill thought, *This man is from out of state. Maybe he can help jog my memory somehow.* He said, "Mr. Gorham, would you like to join me for lunch aboard my houseboat? You'll be treated to Simon's Southern vittles, as he calls them. You'll find them different from what you are used to, but you might take a liking to them. I know I have."

After lunch Simon served port on the deck and kept them in stitches with the folklore of the area and personal stories from his past.

When Gorham's guests didn't show up that afternoon, or the next, he decided to go back to the lodge.

"Mr. Sutton, how would you like to come to the lodge with me?" Gorham asked. "We could hunt quail and duck, assuming you like to hunt."

"I'd love to," said Bill. "Let's take the houseboat and tow yours. I eventually planned to go up the sound anyway and stop off at the home of Fernie Taylor, a friend I met at Mrs. Willis' boardinghouse. He visited me aboard the houseboat several times and invited me to visit him on his plantation. It will save you from having to bring Simon and me back to Beaufort."

George agreed and they left that afternoon. Several hours later they tied up at the hunting lodge dock. Bill spent a few days with his new friend, then he and Simon left for the Taylor plantation.

CHAPTER ELEVEN

Delia named the baby William Sutton Jr. after his father, and nicknamed him Will. The day he turned three, Miss Lucy and Delia sat on the piazza and watched him play with a little red wagon Delia had ordered for his birthday.

"Chile, that youngern needs a father," said Miss Lucy. "Toby didn't have one, Gaud rest his soul. I'm going to the lifesaving station and send a message to the sheriff in Beaufort and ask him has he laid eyes on that Yankee of yern."

She took her crooked walking stick and, with Sooner following, headed down the narrow sandy path that wound around the lake to the lighthouse. Sooner ran on ahead. Finding the telegraph shack door open, he snuck inside undetected by the telegraph operator, climbed up a ladder leaning against the wall, and made his way down a rafter directly over the operator's head. Sooner could be devilish at times. In fact, he was good at playing pranks on people. He had learned to wait for the right moment to make a certain type of sound for maximum effect when he snuck up on someone. Without warning, he could utter a kind of high-pitched, ear piercing staccato noise that usually elicited sheer panic from anyone not expecting it. When he did it this time, the frightened young telegraph operator let out a yell, jumped up, knocked his chair over, dove out the window, and dashed around the corner of the shack, yelling, "Skunk! Skunk!" He collided with Miss Lucy, knocked her down, and fell on top of her.

"Dammit, ye clumsy oaf. Ye pert' near knocked the wind outta me. And that ain't a skunk. He is a raccoon."

The man helped her to her feet and started to apologize when Miss Lucy stopped him. "Get in that shack and start clicking out a message I want sent."

"Lady, I'm not allowed to send personal messages. Government rules state this telegraph is for lifesaving emergencies only."

"You'll send my personal message or otherwise I'll mellow yer head with my walking stick. Ye ain't been stationed here long, or ye would know I'm Miss Lucy Jenkins. I ain't called Queenie fer nothing—of course that's when I'm not around. Now get to that dit-dot machine, and send this message to Sheriff Haskins in Beaufort. Ask him has he seen a queer looking vessel called a houseboat and a man named Bill Sutton."

With Sooner still in the rafters over his head, and Miss Lucy looking over his shoulder, the Morse code operator appeared nervous and tentative while sending the message that said, "Have you seen a queer boat with a vessel named Bill Sutton?"

The sheriff sent a return message: "Are you off in your rocker? Reply with a sane message."

The sheriff's second message read: "A man with amnesia named Bill Sutton and his boatman, Simon, left Beaufort aboard an unusual vessel heading south days ago."

On her way home Miss Lucy stopped to rest her aching hip. Removing her shoes, she waded out from shore to a large tree limb hanging over the water, and sat dipping snuff as she marveled at the way Sooner could crack open oysters and suck out the small morsels. *Now I know why they got the name coon oysters,* she thought.

Miss Lucy was enjoying watching minnows play around her feet when suddenly the blast of a ship's horn ripped through the air. Looking up, she saw a vessel under full sail coming through the mouth of Silver Lake.

"Gaud a'mighty!" she yelled. "That fool will surely run her high and dry afore he can strike her sails." The vessel continued swiftly toward her. She jumped from her perch, called Sooner, and started ashore just as the vessel made two sharp turns to slow its momentum. This created two large wakes that washed ashore, wetting Miss Lucy to her waist. Oblivious to the soaking, she stood staring at the name on the ship's bow. "Can't be!" she said. "But, by Gaud, thar it is. *Sweet Thang 2* is written as plain as day across her bow. We thought she sank, taking Captain Urah Wayhab and his crew to the bottom of the ocean with her."

Delia worried about Miss Lucy being gone so long, and left the house to look for her. She met her hurrying down the path with her shoes in her hand and holding her wet dress to her knees.

"Oh my God! Miss Lucy, did you fall overboard?" she asked.

"No. See that ship lowering its anchor? Well, its wake caught me afore I could get out of the way. It's Urah Wayhab, my old beau. He has finally come home. Jest you wait 'til I get my hands on that rascal. He left here with a hull full of turpentine heading for the Virgin Islands and wasn't heard of 'til today."

"Why, Miss Lucy, you never told me you had a beau . . . and how do you know it's him?" Delia asked.

"It's him all right, no one but Urah Wayhab could bring a vessel into the lake under full sail and with the wind blowing off her stern. 'Sides I saw *Sweet Thang 2* on her bow." She paused, thinking, *Why Number 2 and not 1?* Then she continued, "Many years ago, Urah's wife died a couple of years after my man did. Well, we sorta became sweet on each other. Come, I want to get back to the house and change out of these clothes. 'Sides, I have something to tell ye, then we'll go meet Urah. It will be a while before he comes ashore."

Back at the house, Delia made tea while Miss Lucy changed into dry clothes. Going into the kitchen, she asked Delia to sit down. "I have some good news and I have some bad news. The good news is Bill left Beaufort days ago heading up Bogue Sound. The bad news is the reason we haven't heard from him is that he has amnesia."

"My God!" Delia cried, putting her hands over her face. "He's alive, but what am I going to do? How will I ever find him? If I do, will he remember me?"

"Don't ye worry about that now, my dear. At least he's alive, and we know where he's heading. We'll find him somehow. Come, chile, I see folks heading for the pier. Let's join them."

On their way to the pier Miss Lucy explained that it was Urah's first trade mission after the war. His ship, as well as many seagoing vessels along the coast from Wilmington to the Virginia line, was confiscated during the Civil War by the Confederate army. They were put to use—some patrolling the coast and others carrying supplies to army posts stationed up inland rivers.

Delia mingled among the islanders that waited on the pier hoping the dinghy would be bringing their friends and loved ones ashore.

As the boat drew near some of the people began to react. They sobbed, hugged and consoled one another as expectations gradually turned to painful disappointment. It was clear now, as the dinghy approached the pier, that Captain Urah was the only one they recognized. The other five were ruddy-complected strangers. Those expecting to see loved ones gradually drifted away from the pier. Urah saw Miss Lucy and yelled, "Look, me love, what I bring you." He held up a coconut painted with a hideous carved face, and a string of shell beads.

"Urah Wayhab! Ye look like a buzzard's nest and don't ye dare call me ye love, ye rascal. Where in the tarnation have ye been to get sech an ugly thang? I'll not have it in my house."

"I'll tell you all about it later, me love. How about cooking a mess of collards with salted sowbelly and some crackling cornpone? Gaud, how I've missed your good vittles."

Delia thought that Urah resembled some of the rugged-looking seafaring men she had seen on London's waterfront. He had a tall, muscular body, a ruddy face, and his hair and beard were long and white-streaked. Like Miss Lucy, she was anxious to hear about Urah's adventure.

That night folks gathered on Miss Lucy's piazza and in her yard. They eagerly waited Urah's story about what happened to their loved ones and friends.

Delia sat on one side of Urah and Lucy sat on the other as Urah gave an account of his seven years of absence.

He told the group he was four days out of Martinique Island when they encountered a hurricane that blew them off course. Three of his crewmen were killed when the masts broke and fell to the deck.

Urah paused and lit his pipe to dead silence, except for the chirping of crickets and a whippoorwill call. Delia and the group sat spellbound until Miss Lucy said, "For Gaud's sake, finish yer spiel."

"We drifted for several days and finally shipwrecked on the reef of an uncharted tropical island. We took what we could salvage from the *Sweet Thang No. 1* wreck and other wrecks that met the same fate. It took several years to make *No. 2* seaworthy enough to make it to St. Kitts Island, where more repairs were made for the voyage home."

"What happened to your last three crewmen?" Delia asked.

"Well, the third day we drifted, one was trying to catch fish with our last salt mullet when a shark grabbed the bait. His foot became tangled in the line and the last we saw were . . . fragments of . . . flesh and blood. Don't anyone dare ask his name, for I alone will carry it to my grave," he said as he bowed his head.

Delia broke the silence that followed when she said, "Mr. Wayhab, that leaves two crewmen. What became of them?"

"They fell in love with native gals and stayed on the island. I promised the natives you saw today that I would carry them home on my next voyage."

Delia thought, *Maybe that's why Urah stayed gone so long. He too, probably had a lady love or two.*

Urah's house, unoccupied since he left on his trade mission, had suffered through several hurricanes and was unlivable. He slept aboard his schooner with the crew, but spent most of his time with Miss Lucy.

A week later, Delia decided she would leave and look for Bill. Urah could then move in with Miss Lucy. She planned to leave soon for Beaufort.

"You can't go to Beaufort, chile," said Miss Lucy. "Not with that purty red hair. The sheriff might still be looking for ye. If'n ye must go, I'll dye it with some pokeberry juice. It will come out the first time ye wash yer hair. We also use it for ink." The purple juice turned her red hair into a mousy brown color.

Miss Lucy stood on the dock waving her handkerchief as Delia and Will left the dock in a small sailboat with Urah at the helm. Before the boat was out of sight she left the dock, crying. Delia promised her that she would return some day, with her husband or without.

It was dusk when Urah put them ashore on the outskirts of Beaufort. Being familiar with the way to Shantytown, she soon knocked on Preacher Thomas' door. It was several minutes before she heard feet shuffle toward the door.

"Who's thar?" asked Lizzie. When she was told it was Delia, she cried, "Praise the Laud! She is alive. Thomas, it's Delia! She's alive."

Delia embraced Lizzie and saw Preacher Thomas and a strange black man sitting by the window. The preacher held a Bible in one hand and a magnifying glass in the other. She kissed him on the cheek, and could tell her friends' health had failed since she left them. "How are you both since I last saw you?" she asked.

"I have lots of misery in my knees and arms," said Lizzie, "and Thomas had a slight stroke a few years back. He jest a part-time preacher now, but still does a little yard work for Cap'n Willis."

"Did Rufus get away to Charleston?" Delia asked.

"Yes, and he told us about the baby dying. We were so sad for you and the baby," said the preacher. And po' Mrs. Sara, she went to her grave not believing any of those mean things people said about you."

"But tell me, Miss Delia, who's this fine-looking young man?"

"This is my son Will, short for William Sutton. He'll soon be four."

Delia then related to Lizzie and Preacher Thomas the events that had occurred since she last saw them.

When she finished the preacher introduced the stranger by the window, who had been ignored since she entered the room.

"This is Fairlee, a cousin of mine from Wilmington, but he lived most of his life in Morehead City. He has to leave soon and was about to tell us about the time he cooked for the Yankees when he was a prisoner at Fort Macon."

"I would like to hear your story, Fairlee," said Delia, pulling a chair up beside Lizzie.

Fairlee's grandmother had raised him and taught him how to cook. Later, he joined the Confederate Army and served as a cook at several army posts before being transferred to Fort Macon with his company soon after it was built.

"We hardly settled in befo' we were captured by the Yankees and put in our own prison. Someone tol' dem I was a good cook and they put me in the kitchen. The fust day the man in charge tol' me to put salt peter in the vittles. I say, 'What fer?' He say, 'To keep the men from being horny.' Dat's when I knew they were loonies."

Delia put her hand over her mouth to keep from laughing. Preacher Thomas hung his head and she could see a smile.

"I had a plan. I tol' dat man I need some bay leaves from outside the fort. Instead I plucked a bag of caster beans. Dat's what caster oil made from. Dat night I crushed 'em and put 'em in a pot of black-eyed peas, and sent word to the prisoners not to eat the peas." He stopped long enough to spit tobacco juice into the spittoon.

"Well, it wasn't long befo' all hell broke loose. I never seen sech a sight. They ran out of the barracks, yelling, 'Open the drawbridge!' Dat's the only way in or out of that fort. Some

126

was in their long johns and some was tripping over their britches suspenders, heading for the drawbridge. I ran right along with dem—they was so busy they didn't ever know I was thar."

Delia couldn't contain her laughter any longer and the preacher and Lizzie burst out laughing along with her.

"I ain't through," Fairlee said. "I crossed dat bridge and kept right on trotting. Found me a skiff and rowed to Beaufort, where I was hid by white folks until the war was over. I was a hero, they said."

"Thanks Fairlee," Delia said. "I haven't laughed that much in a long time."

Preacher Thomas arranged for Delia and Will to go to Morehead with a man he knew that sold oysters and scallops every Friday to a seafood market, a café, and several boarding-houses in town. From Morehead she could catch the freight boat up Bogue Sound to Swansboro.

Early the next morning they left to meet Sam Dixon, the man that would take her and Will to Morehead. Two miles out of Beaufort, Preacher Thomas turned the old mule and cart down a path of crushed oyster shells that finally ended at a small estuary on Newport River. A man stood by a small shack waiting for them.

Delia was horrified when she saw the small boat that would take them to Morehead. It was filled to the gunwales with sacks of oysters. She thought it would sink when they stepped aboard, but Dixon assured her it would not sink and that he needed to leave now and cross the channel early, because he didn't want to run into the wakes of larger boats and take on water.

The thought of taking on water was still on Delia's mind as they pulled away from shore. Her determination to find Bill helped keep her thoughts focused on the immediate task at hand. The laughter of Will at what was occurring above them provided badly needed levity to her predicament. He was amused at a flock of sea gulls making their high-pitched laughing sounds as they swooped and dived in the sky above them. Apparently the gulls mistook the sacks of oysters, with their strong smell, for fish, and were looking for a meal.

Delia and Will were put ashore on the waterfront of Morehead, near the moored mail boat that also carried freight. After paying twenty cents for the trip down Bogue Sound, they were helped aboard and seated among all sorts of cargo to be delivered at several docks along the way.

One passenger introduced himself as Captain Dexter and said he was with the lifesaving station at Bogue Inlet. He was holding a bottle of booze, already tipsy, and talked continuously. "I'm celebrating a release from court for being accused of killing a seventeen-year-old boy while chasing Katie Bowen, a moonshine runner. We been trying to catch her for two years, but she always gave us the slip until the day we saw her boat leave a cove on the beach."

He stopped yapping long enough to take a swig from his bottle, then he rattled on, much to Delia's dismay. She whispered in Will's ear, "Don't say anything, and maybe he will hush."

"We chased her, came alongside and gave the order to stop three times. Instead, she opened full throttle. I shot over her bow as a warning, missed, and killed the boy. The boat, out of control, ran ashore, but she had disappeared. The rumor around Swansboro is she swam ashore and somehow made it to New York, where she opened a brothel and became wealthy selling branch water and moonshine that is secretly shipped to her from someplace on the east coast."

"Watch that waterspout forming dead ahead," the captain shouted. "Put on your life vests and hold on to your seats. If it doesn't break up before it reaches us I might have to run her ashore to avoid it."

Oh God, what is going to happen to me next? thought Delia. She watched transfixed as the dark funnel spout seemed to scorch the top of the water, creating a white spray as it sucked up more water. It continued its rapidly swaying motion toward them. The captain turned the boat toward Bogue Banks just as the waterspout struck the boat broadside, filling it with water. When it slowly began to sink, Delia grabbed Will and jumped overboard into waist-deep water. *Thank God,* thought Delia, *we are near shore.*

She took Will in her arms and sloshed ashore onto Bogue Banks. Looking back, she saw the captain and Dexter still in the sound, making their way to the mainland side.

She tried to stay calm for Will's sake, although her emotions were at a breaking point. *What do we do now? Which way do I go?* she thought. Then she remembered Mr. Dexter saying he worked at the lifesaving station on Bogue Banks. She decided to try to make her way there.

They walked along the narrow shoreline toward the setting sun. She barely noticed the occasional blue crab dashing for safety from the shallow water or the flounders scurrying from the sanctity of their beds as she stepped over and around fallen trees and driftwood.

The sun dipped behind the trees as they rounded a point and saw a small dock jutting out into the sound. They followed a small footpath that ran inland from the dock to several small houses, obscured by trees and tall bushes.

Breaking clear of the path, they saw four men busy doing something with barrels. The men didn't see them until several hound dogs darted from beneath a porch and raised a ruckus, restrained only by the chains around their necks. It turned out the men had different tasks. Some were putting hoops around barrels, while others were cutting holes near the bottom and inserting wooden pegs where spigots would go. They stopped working and stared when they saw Delia and Will. An elderly man appeared with a shotgun in the doorway of one of the houses. When he saw it was just a woman and a boy, he called off the dogs.

"You mustn't slip up on folks like that," he said. Then, turning to the men, he assured them, "Everything's all right, boys. It's just a gal and a young boy."

The man turned his attention back to Delia and asked, "Where did you come from gal, and how did you happen to find us?" Delia thought he appeared apprehensive. She explained about the waterspout, the sinking of the freight boat, and how they made their way along the shore until they saw the dock.

"Aye, so it swamped you, did it? We saw it and it was a big one. I'm glad I wasn't in its path. By the way, my name is Bennie Bowen, and we are all relatives living here. Have a seat on the porch while I put this gun in the house."

When he went inside, Bill whispered to Delia, "Mama, his name is the same as that liquor runner woman Captain Dexter told us about."

"Shhh . . . I know. Don't mention what Captain Dexter told us or we might be in trouble. I'll ask the man if we can spend the night. It'll soon be too dark to see our way."

The man returned and Delia inquired into the possibility of spending the night.

"We have just one bedroom. I will have to ask my wife, Bell, when she comes from the sti—I mean back from across the way. She is awful jealous, and you are a good-looking redhead."

It was the first time Delia realized the water had washed the pokeberry juice from her hair.

The men in the yard were listening to their conversation and one of the younger men said, "I live alone, so she can stay with me."

The rest of the men laughed. "Hush your mouth, Jed," Bennie said. "And hurry and finish hooping those barrels. We will need them tonight."

Bell returned smelling of corn mash, and was about to refuse to let them spend the night when Delia said she would pay her for the night's lodging. Reaching in her brassiere, Delia pulled out a dollar. Bell reluctantly took the money. "We have two rooms—a bedroom and a kitchen. The boy can sleep in the kitchen and you can sleep in the woodshed. And don't go wondering around the place. Supper will be ready in an hour."

Delia was almost certain she and Will had discovered the suppliers of Katie Bowen's moonshine.

Bell served a delicious supper of stone crab claws and clam fritters. Afterwards, Delia helped Bell clean the kitchen and put up the cot for Will. He had fallen asleep at the table.

Taking the kerosene lamp and an old blanket Bell gave her, she started for the woodshed. In the moonlight she saw the men, carrying the barrels they were working on, disappear behind a sand dune.

She pushed open the rusty-hinged door and closed it behind her. Moving pieces of stove wood, she spread the blanket on the hard dirt floor, and soon fell asleep.

Just before dawn she was awakened by the screech of the rusty hinge. Thinking it might be Will, she called his name twice. When no one answered, she picked up a piece of stove wood and waited. Suddenly, she felt a hand on her leg and smelled the pungent odor of liquor. Angry and scared, she struck as hard as she could with the stove wood and heard a crack, then a scream, followed by a man's voice. "You bitch, you broke my arm."

Lighting the lamp, she discovered it was the same man that had offered her his house for the night.

"You make one move toward me and I'll break your head. Now get out of here, you bum."

Bennie heard the commotion and, afraid he would wake Bell, slipped out of bed and ran to the woodshed. Jed was rolling around on the floor and Delia was standing over him with a stick of stove wood.

"She broke my arm," Jed said when he saw Bennie. "And after she told me to meet her here for a little pleasuring."

"Stop your lying," said Bennie. "She should have broken both arms." Taking Delia aside, he whispered, "Gal, its best you leave before sun-up. He's Bell's nephew and all the womenfolk will take up for him. I will go fetch the boy and a few provisions."

Bennie returned with Will, food from the previous night's supper, a box of matches, and a jug of water.

"How far is Bogue Inlet Lifesaving Station?" she asked.

"About five miles, I reckon," Bennie said, scratching his head. "I've never been there."

With the moon as their guide, they slowly picked their way along the sound side of the island. The sunrise and low tide helped make walking toward their destination easier.

They were several miles up the island when a sow and a litter of pigs darted from the water into the underbrush. Will dropped the shells he had gathered and went chasing after them.

"Will Sutton, you get back here!" yelled Delia. "You don't know what might be in there." When he didn't answer or appear, she went up the overgrown trace to find him. He was standing on the edge of a large pond surrounded by white sand, staring at a small cabin that was almost hidden behind myrtle bushes and fox grapevines.

"Hello! Anyone there?" she hollered twice. Receiving no answer, she grabbed Will's hand and gingerly walked around the pond toward the cabin. Peeking through a small window, she saw spider webs extending from the rafters to the dusty rough floor. "This place hasn't been occupied for a long time," she said.

"Let me see!" cried Will. She held him up to the window. "Oh, Mama, let's go inside."

Delia forced a wooden latch on a wide plank door. The one room was empty except for duck decoys in one corner, foul weather gear hanging from a peg on the wall, and several cane fishing poles leaning against the wall.

"Oh Mama, let's stay here tonight. Maybe I can catch a fish."

"We might as well. It'll be dark before we can reach the lifesaving station."

Using a branch from a wild bay bush, Delia cleaned the room of spider webs and swept the dust from the floor.

For most of the night, Delia lay awake on the hard floor listening to the sawing sounds of the katydids, the croaking of bullfrogs and the mournful sound of a whippoorwill. She thought of her past and wondered if she did the right thing to leave Conch Island in search of Bill. She put her arm around the sleeping Will, and whispered in his ear, "It's not been all bad, my son. I have you."

EPILOGUE

Back on Bogue Banks

Delia sat with her head bowed and said no more. When the silence became oppressive, Fernie cleared his throat and said, "My dear, may I call you Delia?"

"Yes sir, please do."

"Well, Delia," Fernie said, smiling. "I have a nice man visiting me by the name of Bill Sutton, but he . . ."

"Oh God!" Delia screamed, putting her hands to her teary face. "I've finally found him. Can I go to him now?"

"I think it's best if I go home and bring you a change of clothing. I'll go home and bring you one of Caroline's dresses. You'll need needle and thread to take a tuck here and there, as she is larger than you in the wrong places. I'll return early tomorrow morning."

It was almost dark when he returned home. Easter, the black maid, met him at the door. "You's back mighty late, Mr. Fernie. Where has you been? Miss Caroline done eat her supper. She waited fer you long enough."

He ignored her and told her to bring him one of Caroline's dresses and a needle and thread. Easter put her hands on her large hips and frowned. "Mr. Fernie, what's you's up to? Has you's been messing around with some hussy and got her in trouble?"

"It's a surprise," Fernie said, and laughed. "You will soon see—now get the dress. And don't mention this to Caroline or Bill Sutton, or I will send you packing."

"If'n I don't find out what you wants dat dress fer by tomorrow night, I'm sure going to tell on you. Men! Bah! They is all cut from the same cloth," Easter muttered as she left the kitchen.

The next morning Fernie returned to the island and found Delia drying her hair while Will chased bullfrogs back into the pond.

Delia was delighted with the emerald green dress he brought her. "It will go well with my hair. Redheads can wear green," she said, smiling.

"While you dress," Fernie said, "Will and I will go across to the ocean and try some drum fishing."

They returned an hour later with several drums they caught. Delia was dressed and wore a tiara in her hair made from honeysuckle blossoms.

"You look very lovely, my dear," Fernie said. "If seeing you doesn't shake Bill out of his amnesia, nothing will. If you are ready, we can go. Will, you take the fish we caught to Easter. She will be at your beck an' call from now on. That darkie loves fish."

It was early afternoon when they left for the mainland. Will helped Fernie pole the skiff across the sound while Delia sat in the back and cogitated. *What would she say when they meet? Would it be possible for him to remember her?*

Delia kept searching for Bill's houseboat. Finally she asked, "Mr. Taylor, I have been looking for Bill's boat. Where is it?"

"Simon anchored it up Sandy Creek for security reasons before he went back to Beaufort. It's not visible from the sound."

The plans they made were for Fernie and Will to go ahead to the house while Delia waited for Bill on the footpath. Fernie would send Bill back under the pretext that the houseboat needed to be pumped out because of a faulty bilge pump. He would tell Caroline that Will was the son of a friend who was fishing on the beach and who he had invited home to spend the night.

It seemed like hours to Delia as she waited for Bill behind a vine-covered oak tree. "Oh God, please let him recognize me," she whispered over and over. Then she heard the sound of Bill whistling as he drew near. When he was abreast of the tree, she stepped in front of him. Bill fell backward, hitting his head on a stump. He was momentarily knocked unconscious.

She ran to him, cradling his head in her arms. "Oh my God, Bill, are you hurt?" she screamed.

Several moments passed before he opened his eyes and stared at her.

"Lady, you almost caused me to have a heart attack."

She threw her arms around him. "Oh Bill, don't you remember me?" she cried. "It's Delia."

He sat up, rubbed the back of his head, and stared at her with a blank look. "I'm sorry, lady, but I don't. Where did you come from?"

He didn't remember her. She stepped back, put her head in her hands, and felt like the world was crumbling around her. The situation was out of her hands. There was nothing she could do.

The silence was overwhelming. Then a bird flew above them screeching: *kli-li-li-li.* *It couldn't be,* thought Delia. But there it was again: *kli-li-li-li.* They both looked up as a bird flew over their heads and disappeared over the sound.

"Bill! Remember that bird's song?" Delia cried.

"Oh, it's just a bird flying over."

"Yes, but don't you remember, Bill? Miss Lucy's omen. Please remember, Bill! The curlew—our wedding. It made the same call the moment we jumped the broomstick. Miss Lucy said it was a good omen when it cried while in flight. Remember?"

Bill was silent for what seemed like an eternity to Delia. He finally said, "Who's Miss Lucy? What is this superstition about a bird?" Again there was silence. His face showed confusion. He sat on the log with his hands over his face and began to mutter, "Curlew . . . curlew . . . wedding . . . Miss Lucy—my God, my God!"

He stopped, raised his head, and looked at Delia with tears in his eyes. He didn't have to say anything. She knew he remembered. "Oh Delia, my dear," he muttered softly.

With their arms around each other, Bill struggled to recall more and more of the past, while Delia patiently tried to mention mutual experiences that might trigger more recall on Bill's part.

They walked along the path holding hands, oblivious to direction or destination. Delia thought of the event that just took place and questioned her earlier beliefs. Then she said, "You know dear, maybe all of this was meant to happen."

Bill kissed her and said, "No darling, you made it happen. You remembered the bird and made me remember."

"Maybe so," she said, but thought, *I wonder if the curlew had something to do with it.*

The winding path led them to the houseboat, where they sat on the boat's narrow balcony facing Bogue Sound and watched mullets jump in the moon's rippling reflection. Delia brought Bill up to date on all that happened on Conch Island during his absence, with the exception of the tragic loss of his son Toby and his sister's death. She would tell him that later; she didn't want to say something that would end Bill's state of euphoria.

Bill, with his head down, remained quietly cogitating. After a short time he said, "I can't believe all that happened. I am so sorry that I was the cause of all the hardship you experienced. As Miss Lucy would say, you've been momicked."

"Shhh," said Delia, putting a finger to his lips. "The important thing is that we've found each other, and it hasn't all been bad. You know the young boy that went home with Mr. Taylor?"

"Yes, he seemed to be a nice chap with pretty red hair."

"Well, my dear, he is your son."

For several seconds Delia was uneasy as Bill just stared at her, transfixed. The only sound heard was the clang of the bell buoy near Bogue Inlet. Suddenly he sprang up and grabbed her around the waist, lifting her feet clear of the deck. He swung her around so hard that he lost his balance and they fell overboard. They surfaced facing each other and laughed. Bill kissed her. "My God, darling, it's been the most wonderful day of my life."

In the wee hours of morning they drifted off to sleep, their arms around each other. Again they were on Silver Lake, listening to waves gently slap the side of the houseboat.